MR. SEPTEMBER

HEROES OF ROGUE VALLEY: CALENDAR GUYS

BOOK 9

ANN ROTH

Published by Oliver-Heber Books

0 9 8 7 6 5 4 3 2 1

 Created with Vellum

1

"**Y**ou did *what*?" Kylie Treadwell gaped at her older sister Cheryl, who'd stopped by Kylie's apartment with startling news.

Cheryl sat forward in the easy chair and beamed the way a mother would. Nothing new there. "That's right, I won a date with Ethan Goldberg at the fundraiser for struggling musicians. Can you believe it?"

That wasn't much of a stretch. Kylie's sister was beautiful—nearly five feet ten, with green eyes and dimples in her cheek, and blessed with a poise she envied. "Get to the part about transferring the date to me."

"I had to. After all, I'm a happily married woman with a four-year-old son, and I want to stay that way. So I substituted your name and phone number. You're welcome."

"You couldn't check with me first?"

Cheryl's clear excitement deflated like an air

mattress with a nail hole. "I don't even rate a thank you? This is *Ethan Goldberg* we're talking about, Mr. September on the firefighter calendar that hangs in your kitchen and the sax player for one of the hottest bands in town. No available woman in her right mind would turn down the chance to spend an evening with him."

"I would. At the very least, I need to meet a man before I decide whether I want to go on a date with him. Anyway, a popular guy like Ethan would never look twice at regular old me, let alone ask me out."

"Regular?"

"My life isn't exactly exciting. I go to work, I come home. I live a quiet, ordinary life, and I'm content. And you know why."

"Gordon Strand. Yada yada. That was three years ago."

"You weren't the one whose name was dragged through the news for weeks while the police questioned me and searched for him." Gordon, Kylie's live-in boyfriend at the time, had embezzled money from the bank where he worked and fled to Rio. There, he'd taken up with a redhead and blown through the money in record time. Forty thousand dollars, gone.

Her sister waved her hand. "Gordon's in prison and you were cleared of any wrongdoing."

"Yes, but the scars remain." Believing Gordon wanted the same things she did, to build a life together, then finding out otherwise in the most awful way had hurt. "And don't forget what dear old Mom pulled before that."

"Believe me, I won't. But you were ten, Kylie, now you're thirty. It's not like you're going to a drunken brawl. This is completely aboveboard. Ethan agreed to have dinner with you as a way to raise money for the fundraiser."

"Does that sound fun to you?"

"How will you know unless you go? You're wonderful and adorable, and he can't help but like you."

Five feet six with hazel eyes and flyaway dish-water-blond hair hardly qualified as adorable. Kylie rolled her eyes.

"Besides, you haven't had a date in way too long," Cheryl added. "Don't you think it's time?"

"That's up to me, not you."

Kylie gave her sister a dirty look, which she ignored. "A nudge in the right direction can't hurt."

With her traumatic past, who could blame her for being in a dateless rut? Her whole life was one big rut, which was what she wanted. Not really. As grateful as she was for her job as a claims adjuster at Coleman's Auto Insurance, which was stable and paid decently, there were times when she wanted to chuck it all and try something different. Even if the thought gave her hives.

She certainly wasn't going to talk to Cheryl about that. Knowing her sister, she'd probably run out and enroll Kylie in a seminar about finding your bliss without fear. Gag.

Since conquering her own fears through a similar seminar some years ago and subsequently starting a successful business with her own line of soaps, Cheryl was a firm believer in that kind of thing. No, thank you.

She gave Kylie a funny look. "The past few minutes your expression has changed from disgusted to scared to excited to nauseated. What in the world is going through your mind?"

"Dinner with Ethan Goldberg. You've already written the check to the musicians fund, right?" Cheryl nodded. "Then there's no need for the actual date. I'm going to give us both a break and cancel."

"Don't you dare. The details have already been set up. Saturday at seven p.m."

Kylie frowned. "But you and I made plans for a sisters' night out that evening. Dinner and whatever, remember?"

"We'll do it another time. You're keeping this date."

"Yes, Mom," Kylie grumbled. "Where are we supposed to meet for this meal?"

"He's picking you up here at your house."

"You gave him my address?"

"For goodness' sake, it's no secret. You're in the phone book."

Apparently, Kylie was stuck. She blew out an

exaggerated breath. "Where are we going and what am I supposed to wear?"

"I have the information right here." After rifling through her gargantuan purse, Cheryl extracted a sheet of paper and read aloud. " 'The winner will enjoy a gourmet dinner with Ethan Goldberg at the Hearthstone Restaurant, located at beautiful Guff's Lake Resort.' "

That didn't sound half bad, and Kylie had always wanted to eat there. "I'll need something dressier than office attire," she mused, already running through the color-coordinated outfits in her closet in her mind.

"How about that gorgeous navy silk dress with the cream piping? The one you wore to Dad's third wedding."

Now, a scant fourteen months later, the marriage that was supposed to be "the charm" was in its last gasps. Kylie really liked the dress but hadn't had a chance to wear it since. "May as well."

"Do you want me to come over and help you with your hair and makeup?"

"Don't push it, Cheryl. This isn't a real date and I don't expect to enjoy myself."

"At least you're going."

~

AFTER SEVERAL HECTIC weeks battling summer fires and handling numerous emergency calls, the Guff's Lake Fire Department was having a slow day. The leisurely pace matched the oppressive end-of-August heat.

Ethan did his assigned chores. During mid-morning break he walked to Rosemary's Breakfast Nook a few blocks away and bought himself coffee and a scone. Later he worked out at the station's gym with several crewmates.

Mid-afternoon, they split up to do their own thing. Armed with a spiral notebook and the good-luck pen a songwriter friend had once given him, Ethan sat down at the table in the firehouse kitchen and worked on a new song.

Thirty minutes later he'd scribbled six lousy lines, crossed out four, and filled the margins with doodles of stick figures playing musical instruments. Frustrated, he capped the pen and shut the notebook.

What the hell was wrong with him?

What should have been easy—writing the lyrics for Rafe and Jillian's song, his wedding gift to them—had turned into one giant headache. A big waste of time and effort.

For the first time ever he'd hit a creative wall. The muse he'd always taken for granted had been AWOL for weeks, throwing a wrench into his plan to surprise his teammate and soon-to-be wife with something unique and really special.

Nothing, not relaxing with the guys outside work, dating, or playing the sax helped. He was beginning to think he'd never write a decent song again. Where had his inspiration gone and how did he get it back?

Daniel, Rob, and Liam sauntered in and joined him at the table.

"You look like you want to punch something," Liam said.

Ethan snorted. "I would if it'd help me write the words for Rafe and Jillian's song."

"What if you figured out the music part first?"

"I tried that too. It's always been easier for me to start with the words then write the music."

"The wedding isn't until early October. That's a ways off yet."

"Six and a half weeks to write the lyrics and the music, then record it—all between back-to-back shifts here and the concerts on weekends. That's barely enough time."

"You don't have a gig this weekend—unless you call your date Saturday night a gig. Hard to believe you volunteered again for the musicians fundraiser." Daniel shook his head. "After what happened last year, I'd be nervous."

Ethan wasn't the only man grimacing. "Gabriella Zoltana—who could forget her?"

She'd won the date and the evening had gone pretty much the same as each of the previous three years. But afterward, Gabriella had chased him like crazy, dropping in at the station, showing up at Rosemary's where he and other crewmates often went for breakfast Wednesday mornings at the end of their back-to-back shifts, and otherwise dogging him for weeks.

"I handled it," Ethan said.

"You only had to remind her a thousand times that you weren't interested." Smirking, Liam rubbed his shaved head. "She had a real thing for you. Nothing new there except that it took awhile before she got the message."

Ethan shrugged. "Can I help it if the ladies like me?"

His crewmates snorted. He hadn't always been this popular. Throughout high school he'd been puny, shy, and clueless. No girl, even the outcasts, had wanted to hang with him. Ditto with most of the boys. They considered him a dork, and rightly so.

The summer after graduating he'd grown a foot and filled out. When he entered community college in the fall, his fellow students looked at him differently, a real ego boost. Always interested in music, he'd started a band and for the first time girls sought him out. Trouble was, inside he was still the same dorky kid. Girlfriends were far and few between, their interest in him quickly fizzling out.

By the time he joined the fire department he'd learned a few things about relationships. Like how to avoid the sting of a breakup. He didn't get too close or too involved. When that happened, his inner dork took over and he said sappy things that turned women off. Why put himself out there again? His personal life improved tenfold, dork days and rejection banished to the past. He'd never looked back.

"You don't have to raise a finger and they throw themselves at you," Rob said. "Why go out with a woman you've never seen and don't even know?"

"Doing my part to raise funds for a good cause. I've been lucky—Mello is popular and we're making money. Meanwhile, there are plenty of decent musicians struggling to survive. Treating a woman to a dinner is my way of thanking her for her contribution. I show her a nice time, we get a decent meal, and she goes home happy. The next morning she gets a memento of the evening—a photo and an article in the Sunday paper, print and online."

"Do you know anything about her?" Rob asked. "What's her name?"

Ethan couldn't remember. Raising his hip, he pulled his wallet from his back pocket and extracted the form containing the information. "Kylie Treadwell. She's a thirty-year-old auto insurance claims adjuster."

Which was all he needed to know. They'd spend only a couple hours together before going their separate ways.

"Kylie Treadwell—where do I know that name from?" Liam rubbed his chin.

"Beats me, but it does sound familiar." Ethan checked his watch. "It's my night to cook and if you guys don't eat on time, all hell will break loose. I'd best get to it."

2

S tanding in front of the full-length mirror in her bedroom Saturday evening, Kylie studied herself with a critical eye. Navy was a good color on her, bringing out the green in her hazel eyes and making her skin look creamy. The dress fit her curves without going overboard, and the heels on her silver sandals added three inches to her height. The shoes were less than comfortable—the straps rubbed her pinky toes—but in an hour or two, max, she could take them off.

After tucking a loose lock of hair into place she added a touch more lipstick. "Not bad," she told her reflection.

Although why she bothered when she didn't care at all about impressing Ethan Goldberg was a mystery to her.

All right, he was attractive. Super attractive, but he'd never know she thought so. Unlike every other woman in town, she refused to draw attention to herself in public or fawn over him.

Even if, like any normal female, she fantasized about the mouth-watering firefighters on the calendar.

A music sensation as well, Ethan stood out even more. At his concerts women reportedly mobbed him. From what Kylie had observed at Lucky Joe's during the one Mello concert she'd attended, he ate up the attention. Photos of him were all over social media.

That kind of recognition and notoriety... Kylie cringed at the thought. She wanted a quiet, ordinary life with a quiet, ordinary man. She'd meant what she'd told Cheryl earlier in the week—she didn't expect to enjoy herself. Still, even if this wasn't a real date it was nice to be going out. Cheryl was right about that. It was time to start dating again.

As Kylie plumped the throw pillows on the sofa so that the living room looked its best, the doorbell rang. Walking slowly so as not to appear eager, she answered the door.

Due to the large crowd at Lucky Joe's she'd only seen Ethan in person from a distance. The calendar photo of him didn't do justice to his rugged side. Tall and tan with fine lines around his eyes, broad shoulders, and a fit, muscled body inside a summer sport coat and pants, he was impossible to resist. And that dress shirt open at the neck...

Inexplicably, she wanted to lick the hollow of his throat. Oh, please.

On a scale of one to ten, he was a fifty. A fact that, judging by his confident smile, he was well aware of.

Refusing to feed his oversize ego, she kept her tongue in her mouth and did her best to appear nonchalant. "Hi," she said, proud of her outward calm. "I'm Kylie."

"Ethan." He shook her hand, his dark eyes combing over her.

Automatically she drew herself up tall and sucked in her stomach. Then catching herself quickly dropped the pose. "Would you like to come in?"

"Sure." He glanced around the living room. "Nice place."

"I like it. I've only been here a few months. I've never lived in a duplex before, let alone a newer building."

"Where were you before?"

"Sharing a two-bedroom apartment across town. My roommate wanted to live with her boyfriend, so I found a new place to live."

"They chased you out?"

"They didn't have to. There's nothing worse than feeling like a third wheel."

"I hear ya."

Kylie doubted he'd ever been in that position. She picked up her shawl. Due to the oppressive heat she hadn't planned on wearing it, but when

Ethan placed it around her shoulders she changed her mind.

He smelled really good. Nothing overpowering, just a hint of man and spice. His fingers brushed her arm and she got goose bumps.

Get a grip.

She opened the door and led the way outside.

"Don't you need to lock up?" he said.

"Yes." In her stupor, she'd forgotten.

Moments later, he opened the door to his SUV and helped her into a luxurious leather seat.

"This is a classy car," she said after he slid into the driver's side. "What kind is it?"

"Cadillac Escalade. It's big enough to hold my band mates and their instruments. Ready?"

No. She felt nervous and a little scared, although she couldn't have said why. Too late—Ethan was already backing out of the driveway.

OTHER THAN MAKING the evening as smooth and painless as possible Ethan hadn't given much thought to tonight's date. Kylie surprised him. He'd pictured a starry-eyed woman thrilled to spend the evening with him, the same as his past fundraiser dates.

Kylie didn't seem that impressed, which was refreshing but also made him wonder what kind of man did. Who was she? "Tell me about yourself, Kylie Treadwell," he said on the thirty-minute drive to the Hearthstone.

"I'm a claims adjuster at Coleman's Auto Insurance."

"I think I read that on the form."

"Form?"

"The one you filled out when you entered the contest at the fundraiser."

"Actually, my sister put my name on her entry."

He hadn't expected that. "Seriously?"

"That's right, she entered me without even asking. She's married and a mom and I'm not, so..."

Ethan chuckled.

"It may seem funny to you, but she drives me nuts," Kylie said. "She's always tried to mother me."

"I have one of those, too. Although when Heather got married she stopped."

"Cheryl's been married six years and still hasn't."

"Is she older or younger than you?"

"Four years older."

"Heather only has a year on me. Maybe that explains it."

"All I know is, Cheryl sticks her nose into my business every chance she gets."

"She does, huh? Maybe your mom puts her up to it. You know, to find out stuff you don't tell her. My mom does that sometimes."

"Not mine. Since she and my dad split up, I don't talk to her much."

She didn't add anything more and Ethan didn't ask. He scrubbed the back of his neck. "I've been doing this four years now, and most of the women enter the raffle because they want a date with me—that and the picture of us in the paper. Sounds cocky but it's a fact. You, though..." He shook his head. "This is a first."

"Back up," she said. "What picture in the paper?"

"You didn't know about that? The reporter who covers these things snaps a few photos at the restaurant and chooses one to go with a short piece in tomorrow's Sunday paper—both the hard copy and the online versions."

She pressed her hand to her lips. Definitely uneasy about the idea. "I don't want my photo in the paper."

Another surprise. "Trust me, it's no big deal," he assured her.

She didn't look at all convinced.

"The people behind the fundraiser insist on the photo and story. It's great PR for them as well as for the Hearthstone."

"You're a local celebrity and a big draw. You like attention."

"Hell, yes. Any mention of Mello and the GLFD is good. What's wrong with having a picture of us in the paper?"

. She shifted in her seat and once again covered her lips with her fingers before she spoke. "I guess I should tell you. After all, it's common knowledge. Do you know who Gordon Strand is?"

Ethan thought a moment. "Isn't he the guy who stole money from the bank where he worked and left the country? To Rio, if I remember right."

"That's him. I was the lucky woman he lived with."

Not at all what Ethan had expected. "Talk about a bum deal. I thought your name sounded familiar. What was he like?"

"Before it happened he seemed like a regular guy. When we moved in together we'd been dating almost a year. I assumed we both wanted the same thing—a future together. Boy, was I wrong." She laughed without a speck of humor.

"Did you have any idea what he was up to, a gut feeling?"

"If I had, believe me, I'd have booted him out and alerted the police. He seemed distant but he'd been moody for months. He'd get irritated when I brought it up, so I let him be. I assumed that whatever was bothering him would pass or he'd finally tell me and go back to being his normal self. That was my second mistake.

"The day he left began like any other. My job started earlier in the morning than his and he liked to sleep as late as possible. When I left for work he was still in bed, and when I came home his things were gone and so was he."

"Without a word? That's harsh."

"Oh, he left a note. 'It's no fun anymore. I'm out of here.' " Kylie snorted. "I had no idea what he'd done until the police contacted me shortly after I got home. Apparently, he'd been stealing from customer accounts for months. A little here, a little there, and depositing the money into his own account."

"Did he steal from you?"

"He didn't dare. I check my account online every day. I'd have noticed and contacted the bank."

"That's something, I guess." Ethan shook his head. "Unbelievable."

"You have no idea. Seeing my name in print over the next few weeks didn't help." With a sigh, she sat back. "That's why I avoid publicity."

"About that—this story in the paper won't be about you or me. It'll be about the musicians fundraiser and how the money benefits deserving musicians. The group needs all the free press it can get and I don't begrudge using a picture of me to give them a boost."

"Maybe if I duck my head... I don't have a choice, right? By the way, sorry to disappoint you, but until my sister won tonight's dinner with you I'd never even heard of the musicians fundraiser, let alone thought about a date with you. If you'd rather not take me to dinner..."

"Are you kidding? I'm looking forward to it."

Oddly enough, he was. Kylie was cute and interesting and he wanted to spend the next couple of hours with her.

"So you're in the auto insurance business," he said as he neared the Hearthstone. "Do you enjoy what you do?"

"I'm good at it and I like the salary and the regular hours. The company has always treated me well. During the whole Gordon mess, they stood by me without question."

"You're loyal to them, and that's cool. But I don't think you're thrilled with the job." At her questioning look he added, "You didn't mention the work itself."

"To tell you the truth, at times it gets pretty boring. Do you like what you do?"

"Love it. I always wanted to be a firefighter. Never imagined I'd make it, though."

"Why not?"

"I was a scrawny kid. Short, with arms about as big around as spaghetti noodles."

She gave him a look of disbelief. "I have trouble believing that."

"It's true. I didn't grow much or bulk up until college."

"That can't have been easy. Kids can be cruel." She looked as though she understood firsthand.

"A little." Slight underexaggeration. The saxophone had been his salvation. If not for music and the marching band, he'd have been suicidal.

"And look at you now—big and muscular with an important job." At last, an admiring look. "Firefighting is such demanding work. Between that and being a star in your own band, you must be incredibly busy. How did you get into music, too?"

"I started in middle school and discovered I was good at it."

"You're a man of many talents. May I ask you something?"

"Shoot."

"How do you juggle two careers?"

There was a question he rarely heard. "There are challenges, but nothing I can't handle. I work at the fire department only on Mondays and Tuesdays. Pulling a double shift, forty-eight hours straight, is no picnic, but I'm able to devote the rest of the week to my music. Works out really well for me. I don't see myself giving up either one."

"That's awesome." She exhaled a wistful breath.

"You're thinking about dual careers," he guessed.

"How did you know?"

"You'd make a lousy poker player. The question and that sigh gave you away. What's this other career?"

"At this point it's more a secret dream. I haven't told anyone, not even Cheryl."

"Now I'm curious." He raised his eyebrows and waited for details.

"It's not that big a deal. The only reason I don't want my sister to know is, she'll be all over me to do something about it."

"You weren't kidding about the mothering thing. I didn't meet your sister at the fundraiser. She was long gone when she won the raffle. " Kylie gave him a sideways look and he added, "I'm saying I won't tell her or anyone else unless it's okay with you."

"I appreciate that. I'd like to open a business that helps people get organized. Closets, drawers, basements—anything that needs decluttering, then set up filing systems to help them stay organized. I want to call it 'Clutter Buster.' "

"Sounds like something everyone needs. I know I could use help. Why don't you do it?"

"If only it was that easy."

"Are you worried about the money, or is it your loyalty to the company that's holding you back?"

"Neither, if I keep my job at Coleman's and run Clutter Buster evenings and weekends."

"Then what's stopping you?"

"I need to think about it, okay?"

Ethan wanted to know more—he liked Kylie and wanted to know everything about her—but she'd gone all prickly. Shouldn't have asked so many questions.

Never mind. With the great meal ahead, a glass or two of wine, and easy conversation, she'd be relaxed and smiling in no time.

3

The Hearthstone Restaurant was every bit as classy as Kylie had heard—linen tablecloths, candles on every table, plush carpet and decor.

The vibe was a little too romantic for tonight's dinner with Ethan, considering they'd met less than an hour earlier. Kylie wasn't going to let that or the balding reporter with the camera who was there stop her from enjoying the evening.

Ethan made that easy. He wasn't at all the stuck-up, full-of-himself male she'd expected. Friendly and easygoing, he asked questions about her life when most men talked about themselves. She'd always felt tainted by the whole Gordon mess, but Ethan seemed more curious than judgmental. He treated her as if she was special, and she liked him for that. Liked him, period.

She felt so comfortable, she hadn't even blinked before confiding in him about her dream of opening Clutter Buster. She gave him points for encouraging her. At the same time, his last question had put her on the defensive. What was stopping her from starting the business? Kylie didn't want to think about it now. "This is my first time at the Hearthstone," she said.

"Is that right? You're in for a real treat."

She shot a wayward glance at the reporter nearby with his camera trained on them. "How many photos is he going to take?"

"I could answer that if Betsy Pappas, the reporter who usually covers these things, was here. She must be off tonight. Is he bothering you?"

"He's distracting."

"Hang on." Ethan rose and approached the reporter. After a few moments of conversation, the man nodded and left.

"What did you do?" she asked.

"Asked him to stop. He's not gone for good—he'll be back to take a few more photos at the end of the meal."

The server, an attractive brunette who looked about Kylie's age, appeared with menus and a pleased expression. "Welcome back, Ethan. I haven't seen you in a while."

"Hey, Larissa." He flashed a grin and the woman all but swooned.

Kylie didn't blame her. Who could resist that charm?

As amiable as you please, he introduced Kylie to her. He chatted Larissa up with the same low-key flirt, all smooth and interested, he'd used on Kylie during the drive here. Larissa lit up just as Kylie had.

He probably treated every female he came in contact with the same effortless warmth.

Should've guessed. No wonder women threw themselves at him.

So much for feeling special. What an idiot she was for letting Ethan affect her so strongly when she knew better. But then, she'd always been a pushover for a male who treated her decently, mistaking his attention for more than it was. Which was one reason she'd put up with Gordon's moodiness.

At least the reporter wasn't around to snap a photo of her looking like one of Ethan's groupies.

"How's that boyfriend of yours?" Ethan asked Larissa.

She lit up. "As a matter of fact, we got engaged this week. You should see the beautiful ring he picked out. I've having it sized now."

"Congratulations. He's a lucky man."

Kylie was ridiculously relieved, which made her feel even more foolish for jumping to conclusions about Larissa, and for caring, period, when she barely knew Ethan. When from what she'd read about him and observed at the concert she'd attended, he treated all women with warmth.

No point wasting her time thinking he was genuinely interested in her. Why should he be? This wasn't even a real date. He was with her tonight solely because her sister had won this dinner at a fundraiser.

She wouldn't forget again.

"Did the Hearthstone live up to your expectations?" Ethan asked as he and Kylie exited the restaurant.

She nodded. "Even better. It's a beautiful place and the food more than lived up to its reputation."

She wasn't half as enthusiastic or warm as she'd been going in. Except for his asking her one question too many in the car, she'd been talkative and open from the time he'd picked her up, a promising start to an evening he'd been less than excited about. As he'd anticipated, she'd relaxed soon after they sat down.

Only to cool toward him again. Something had changed, but damned if he could figure out the cause.

In the soft darkness of evening, tiny white lights twinkled on the branches of the resort's sycamores and oaks, like Disneyland or Christmas, only in late summer. Between the lights and the waxing moon, Kylie was clearly visible. Somber expression, gaze carefully averted, arms hugging her shawl close despite the warm temperature—hardly the picture of happiness.

"You're awful quiet," he said.

"Dinner filled me up, and that skillet chocolate chip cookie totally did me in. With the reporter back for a dessert picture, I thought I should pretend to eat the whole thing. Who am I kidding? It was so scrumptious, I couldn't have stopped if I'd tried. Now I'm too full even to talk." Her lips twitched. "I may never eat again."

That sounded like the Kylie in the car. Relieved, Ethan grinned and patted his belly. "They did feed us well. It's early yet and I could use a walk. How about a stroll along the lake?"

"That's three miles."

"We don't have to go that far. Say the word when you want to quit and we'll turn around and come back."

"These shoes aren't the most comfy and I don't want blisters. Anyway, I should get home. I'm sure you have things to do."

Nothing he couldn't put off. Her message was clear—she didn't want to spend more time with him.

It'd been awhile since a woman had turned down his company and reminded him of high school and community college. But those days were long gone, his inner dork locked up good and tight. He gave a terse nod. "I'll take you home."

In the car, the reason for her distance dawned on him—she had a boyfriend. "Are you involved with someone?" he asked.

She shook her head. "At the moment I'm not even dating."

"A woman like you?"

"What do you mean?"

"You're pretty and you fascinate me."

"Right."

"I mean it. Why aren't you dating?"

"Two words—Gordon Strand."

"I doubt there are many guys around who'd embezzle money from their workplace."

"Let's hope not. Remember, Gordon also left with no warning and took up with another woman without a thought for me. He lied, cheated, and broke my heart."

Caught up in the crime side of the man's life, Ethan hadn't considered that. "He put you through hell, that's for sure. Do you still have feelings for him?"

She looked horrified. "How can you even ask?"

"You said you're not dating."

"It took me awhile to get past what happened, but I'm pretty much there now. I don't want to talk about Gordon anymore. Are you involved with anyone?"

"Not seriously. Why, are you interested?"

She rolled her eyes as if to say *no way*. "I answered when you asked me. Now it's your turn."

"I've had my share of girlfriends but nothing that went anywhere. And that's fine. I like my life the way it is—free and single." Firmly in control of his feelings and the things he said to women, a man they gravitated toward. "Heck, I'm only thirty-three. There's plenty of time to settle down later."

That was the end of the conversation. Confused, he tried again as he walked her to her door. "If I offended you in any way tonight..."

"What gave you that idea?"

"Earlier, we were comfortable with each other. We didn't have any trouble making conversation and I thought we clicked. Then something shifted. You're tense."

"I just..." She hesitated. "You did your duty and fulfilled your obligation. I had a good time but I don't expect or want anything more."

"In other words, go away, dude. Got it." Ethan shoved his hands in his pockets.

"You aren't beholden to me, Ethan. You can have any woman you want."

At the moment, he wanted Kylie. "I admit this date started out as an obligation. As soon as I met you I changed my mind. I think you're great." Pleased surprise replaced her disbelief and transformed her face. Wowed, he tucked an errant lock of hair as fine and soft as silk behind her ear. "I got it wrong earlier. You're not pretty, you're beautiful."

She scoffed but didn't move away or lower her gaze from his. "I know a line when I hear it. I've looked in the mirror. I'm not bad, but beautiful?"

"I wouldn't feed you a line—it's not my thing." Now that they'd talked, he figured she'd be open to getting together another time. "I want to see you again. What are you doing Wednesday night?"

"I don't think so, Ethan."

Seriously bummed, he tried a different tack. "Do I at least rate a kiss?"

"So that's what this is about."

"Partly. You heard what I said. I'm a straight talker. No phony stuff."

She scoffed.

"You really don't trust men."

"Do you blame me?"

"We're not all alike. Can I kiss you?"

"If you must."

Despite her indifference, she tilted her head toward him. He cupped her shoulders and brushed his lips over hers. No reaction at first, but a moment later she wrapped her arms around his neck and kissed him back.

Sweetness and a hint of unleashed heat made him want to get closer. He went in for more but she broke away.

Under the porch light, her eyes gleamed with warmth. "Thanks for dinner, Ethan. Good night."

"Night."

He thought about her all the way home.

4

———

Kylie was just waking up Sunday when Cheryl called. "Morning," Kylie said, stretching and sitting up. "If you're wondering about last night, yes—I had a better time than I expected."

"That's obvious."

"You can tell from my voice?"

"Not exactly. Have you seen the Sunday paper?"

"I'm still in bed. Hang on." Kylie shrugged into her robe. Clutching her phone, she padded to the front door. "I'm stepping onto the stoop now to get it."

Another sunny day and already hot. Autumn couldn't come soon enough. She went in again and shut the door behind her. "Okay, I have it. I'm taking it into the kitchen. Give me a minute to start the coffeemaker."

"Forget that and turn to the Arts & Life section."

"Let me guess—there's a photo of Ethan and me at the Hearthstone." Curious, Kylie plunked onto an upholstered stool at the eating bar and found the section. "You could have warned me about the reporter with his camera. If—"

Forgetting what she was saying, she gasped at the two color photos at the top of the page. "I expected to see a picture of us at the Hearthstone. But another of us kissing? How on earth did he manage that? I distinctly remember Ethan saying he was supposed to take pictures at the restaurant only."

"I don't know, but looking at the two of you kissing makes me want to stand in front of the cold air vent."

"Not funny. That was private!"

As upset as Kylie was, seeing herself in Ethan's arms brought it all back. The feel of his solid chest against hers, the seductive press of his mouth making her want more...

Still awed that the magnificent male had held and kissed her, she touched her lips. They actually tingled. She was more amazed that she'd had the wits to pull away.

Even if she liked Ethan, and want to or not she did, he was happy being a ladies' man, which made him all wrong for her.

She was *not* attracted to him. Okay, she was, but she meant to keep that to herself. Or had. She frowned at the paper. "I hope Dad hasn't seen this. He's sure to be thinking about what Mom did. Bad enough I look like her. He'd probably have fits, worrying I'm turning into her. He doesn't like hearing her name, let alone being reminded of what she did. Thank God he doesn't read this section of the paper."

"Dad would never compare you to Mom. Except for the heart-shaped face you don't look anything like her, and personality wise, you're as different from her as day is from night. Plus, they were married when she was photographed dirty dancing with another woman's husband. You're single, fully clothed and standing in front of your door, kissing a very sexy single male most women only dream about. There's no comparison.

"And by the way, Virginia reads that section." Wife number three. "Along with everyone else in town. It's also available on the 'net."

Kylie's head started to pound. She squeezed the bridge of her nose, as if that helped. "What am I supposed to do now?"

"Kiss him again?" Cheryl teased. "You can thank me any time."

"It's not what you think. We were saying good night, period."

Although from the fireworks that had shot through Kylie, her body hadn't gotten the message. After three years of celibacy her libido was alive and kicking.

No wonder she'd failed to hear the click of the reporter's camera or note the flash.

"Did Ethan ask you out for a second date?" Cheryl asked.

"Yes, but I turned him down."

Her sister's shocked breath filled the air. "You turned down a second date with that gorgeous hunk of man? What is wrong with you, Kylie?"

"It'd never work. You've seen his band play at Lucky Joe's. You know how women act when he's around."

"That's not his fault."

"No, but he doesn't exactly discourage the attention. He eats it up. People notice and take pictures and videos, which gets into the papers and is shared all over social media. You know me—I've had way too much of that. I'd rather have a broken arm than be in the spotlight again." Kylie massaged the space between her eyebrows. That didn't help, either. "You should have seen him with our server at the Hearthstone. Turning on the charm, super friendly. She's newly engaged but she was still putty in his hands."

"Define 'super friendly.' "

"Big, warm smile, asking her questions about herself as if she truly mattered to him."

"So he's friendly. Patrick's like that too. Outgoing isn't the same as being interested."

"For Ethan it might be."

"I swear to God, I'd like to slap Gordon's cheating face, and not just because he's a thief. You can't blame Ethan for what he did."

"No, but I'm not about to trust him, either. Why would I? You know how guys are."

"Not all of them. Give the man a chance before you judge him. I would. Oh, to be the woman in his arms... Was that kiss as wonderful as it looked?"

"You'd better hope Patrick isn't listening."

"Believe me, he knows I enjoy the photos of Ethan and the other firefighters on the calendar. He also knows he's the only man for me. About that kiss..." Cheryl prodded.

"Quit being so nosy." Kylie's doorbell rang. "Someone's here," she said, relieved at the interruption. She tiptoed into the living room and peered through a slat in the blinds. "It's Mrs. Crowley from next door," she whispered. "With something wrapped in foil."

"You can bet she wants the scoop on you and Ethan."

Kylie groaned. "I don't want to talk about that with you, her, or anyone else. Shoot, she's seen me. Now I have to answer the door."

"At least you'll get treats out of it. If you tell her more than me, I want to know."

MRS. CROWLEY WAS a seventy-something widow with too much time on her hands. In the few months since Kylie had moved in, she'd had coffee at the woman's house and reciprocated. But never first thing on a Sunday.

"Good morning," Mrs. Crowley looked over Kylie's robe and bed hair. "I hope I didn't wake you."

Kylie tried to look sleepy. "As a matter of fact..."

"You must've been out late." She was practically salivating. "We haven't talked in weeks. I brought you one of my cinnamon loaf coffee cakes to eat while we catch up."

Although Kylie's mouth watered, she resisted. "How thoughtful of you. But I'm barely out of bed and I really do need a shower."

"I won't keep you long. Just tell me about Ethan. When he picked you up last night I thought I'd faint. Such a handsome fellow. I waited up, but you didn't come in until after I went to bed." This time a knowing smile. "And look what I missed. What a kiss."

Embarrassed and appalled, Kylie guided her neighbor out the door. "Everything you need to know is in the article."

"But what about the cake I baked?"

"Another time." The phone chirped. "I need to answer that. Thanks for stopping by."

She made the mistake of picking up without checking the screen.

"Hi, Kylie, this is your dad."

As if she didn't recognize his gravelly voice. "Uh, hi, Dad. What a surprise."

She didn't tell him much more than she had Mrs. Crowley and was trying to get off the phone when a beep signaled an incoming call. This time she did check the screen.

Debbie from work. Odd that she'd call on a Sunday. Must be important. Wrong. Like Kylie's father, Debbie wanted to know about Ethan.

Kylie gave her the same reply before disconnecting. Then she silenced her phone, at last made coffee, and took a mug with her to the bathroom.

After a shower, caffeine, and breakfast, she felt better. When she finally checked her phone mid-afternoon, there were fourteen voice messages and as many texts, all seeking information she wasn't about to give.

She ignored them all except the text from Ethan. Unable to reach u by phone. U ok?

Not by a long shot. Kylie called him.

5

Ethan was out back, sweating in the sweltering heat and getting ready to water his parched lawn when his cell rang. God knew who that was. He slid it from his pocket and checked the screen. Kylie. Well, well.

She hadn't picked up when he'd phoned or replied to his text, and he figured he'd struck out. Seemed he hadn't. Smiling, he answered and headed past the glass sliding doors into his comfy, air-conditioned home.

"I turned off my phone and didn't see your text until now," she said. "It was the only way to get peace."

"I've had calls, too." Most of them while he sat at the desk in his home office staring at the piece of crap that was supposed to be Rafe and Jillian's song. "Crewmates, members of the band, my sister. Before I even opened the paper this morning my mom called. Some photo, huh?"

"I'm surprised, and not in a good way. How did the reporter know where to find us?"

"I'm guessing he waited until we left the Hearthstone and tailed us to your house. By the way, he didn't use a flash when he took that picture, which is why we didn't notice him. A photographer friend explained how to manage it."

"That explains a lot. You're a local celebrity—you're in the paper all the time. People expect to see you kissing one woman or another. No one expects that from me and I don't like it. I didn't want that kind of attention."

"You think I did? The reporter was supposed to get his pictures at the Hearthstone and nowhere else." Trust mattered, ranking right up there with protecting the lives and property of the people in Guff's Lake. Kylie hadn't given him the benefit of the doubt last night and now she probably never would. But he'd try. "We had an end of the evening kiss that was nobody else's business." And had felt like the start of something major Ethan wanted to explore even if Kylie didn't.

"A friendly good night—that's what I told my sister, my dad, my neighbor, and the office manager from work. People I haven't heard from in ages have been calling, texting, and emailing for more information. Isn't there a law about putting photos of people in the paper without their permission?"

"He had permission from you and me both. Your sister signed a waiver when she bought the ticket."

"Of course she did," Kylie muttered.

"I don't share your aversion to being in the news, but I have limits to what I can tolerate. What he did borders on sleazy. I let the managing editor know. Turns out, Betsy Pappas is on medical leave for a few months—the managing editor didn't say why. The reporter who filled in for her is fairly new at the paper. One of his colleagues dared him to get a picture of us at the end of the evening. Both of them have been fired and the editor of the Arts & Life section has been placed on administrative leave. The paper promised to publish an apology tomorrow."

"We'll be in the paper again?" Kylie's groan made him wince.

"They're trying to avoid a lawsuit. I'm not planning to sue, but if you want to..."

"That'll only make it worse."

"None of it will change anything except for my future as a volunteer for the musicians fundraiser. The days of raffling off a dinner with me are over. From now on, I'll donate money, period."

"The fundraiser people are going to be upset."

"Too bad. Thanks to that photo, women will expect me to kiss them at the end of the evening. I don't do that."

"You kissed me."

"That was different. I wanted to."

Silence, except for the sound of Kylie's breathing. "You're thinking about that kiss," he said.

"I am not."

Yes, she was, and they both knew it.

"What are we supposed to do now?" she asked.

"There isn't much we can do, other than wait for things to die down."

Kylie made a sound of disbelief. "With twenty-thousand people in Guff's Lake talking about it and sharing on social media? That won't happen anytime soon. It didn't before."

"The second a bigger story comes along, it will. Trust me on that. As a firefighter and a member of Mello, I've been there. Not the way you have, but I get it."

"Meanwhile, until the next newsworthy thing comes along I still have to face my colleagues at work tomorrow. The comments, questions, speculative looks..." Kylie groaned. "Maybe I'll call in sick."

"That could make matters worse. What you need is a strategy to shut those nosy folks down."

"If you have one, I'm all ears."

"I'll tell you what works for me. Don't make a big deal out of it. You don't owe anyone explanations or answers. Smile or shrug, look them straight in the eyes, and keep your mouth shut. If you do it right, they'll be the uncomfortable ones."

"Great idea— if I can pull it off."

"I have faith in you."

"More than I have. At least I have a partner in crime. No one else understands how stressful this is."

"Yeah." Talking to Kylie was the only good thing about the whole mess, and since they were on a roll... "I was planning to call you even before I knew about the photo," he admitted. "I thought about you all night."

More like fantasized. While that hung in the air between them, he wondered if she'd thought about him too. She'd turned him down for a second date, but after that very hot kiss at her door... Maybe she'd changed her mind. He wanted a chance with her, if only to prove he was one of the good guys.

God knew why that mattered so much, but it did.

"I feel bad about this whole photo mess," he said. "I want to make it up to you."

"If only, but short of going back in time I don't see how. It wasn't your fault the reporter took that picture."

"Good point." He wandered into his office. What a pit. "I wasn't kidding about my home office. It needs major help. If you're willing, the job is yours."

"Are you serious?"

"Totally."

"You do realize you'd be my first paying client."

"That's cool. I'll be able to say I knew you when. How much do you charge?"

"I have it all worked out. I'm going to charge by the hour and my hourly fee will depend on the job."

"Spell that out for me."

"Say you're a hoarder and stuff is piled everywhere. My hourly rate would be a lot higher than if you want to organize the clothes in your closet."

"You've been thinking a lot about this." With the piles of papers everywhere, hiring her could cost a bundle. But he had the money and he wanted the job done. "Sounds reasonable."

"I'll need to see your office before I set the fee."

"Okay." Better tidy up first. He'd have to stash stuff in the garage.

"Do me a favor and don't straighten up in there," she said as if she'd read his mind. "Leave it as is. "

He frowned. "Are you sure about that?"

"Yes. I want a clear picture of how you deal with papers and whatever else you've accumulated. After I look around, I'll draw up a contract with my bid and email it to you."

"Works for me. I'm at the fire station tomorrow through Wednesday morning, but if you're available that evening..."

"I can be. I'll stop by on my way home from work."

"Great. I'll get takeout."

"You don't have to feed me."

"It's no big deal and we both have to eat. Lately I'm into mac and cheese."

"My mouth is already watering. Where do you get it?"

"The Rogue."

"No way. They don't do takeout."

"For me, they do."

"A perk of your fame and fortune?"

He chuckled. "There are one or two."

He gave her his address. When he disconnected, he wore a grin. The week ahead had just gotten a whole lot brighter.

Don't make a big deal out of it. Smile or shrug, look people straight in the eyes, keep your mouth shut. Determined to follow Ethan's advice, Kylie walked into the office of Coleman's Auto Insurance as if nothing had changed over the weekend. As if the paper had never published that second photo.

She also came in earlier than usual to avoid the receptionist and other colleagues. Not all of them. When she reached her desk, Cricket, her counterpart in the adjacent cubicle, was waiting with an extra coffee, an enticing bakery bag, and a winning smile.

"You left here Friday a normal person," she said. "Now, everyone's talking about you. Not like last time, either. More 'Kylie's so lucky.' "

Lucky? Kylie wanted to duck and run. Instead, she shrugged as she imagined Ethan would. "Thanks for the coffee. What's in the bag?"

"Uh-uh. None for you unless you tell me how you got Ethan Goldberg to kiss you."

Forgetting his advice, Kylie glared at her. "In the first place, I didn't 'get' him to do anything. Second, it's none of your business."

"Give a girl a break. I'm only trying to live vicariously through you. It's the closest I'll ever get to kissing a firefighter who also happens to be the sexiest band member of Mello."

Cricket opened the bakery bag and waved it under Kylie's nose. "Samantha's cinnamon rolls, and don't they smell good? They're still warm from the oven. Yum."

"All right! It was a simple thanks at the end of the evening." Except Kylie couldn't stop thinking about the kiss or Ethan—or that she was seeing him again Wednesday night.

"Are you sure that's all there is to it?"

"He's as unhappy about that photo as me. End of story."

"You haven't said if you're going to date him."

Her counterpart's moxie amazed her. She'd

never noticed before. "To repeat myself, end of story. Hand over the bakery bag."

The comments, questions, and looks continued the rest of the day.

As the clock ticked toward closing time, Kylie packed up her briefcase. At five on the nose, relieved to have survived the day, she fled.

A bigger news story couldn't come fast enough.

6

"Coming to breakfast, Ethan?" Rob asked as the crew clocked out Wednesday morning.

After forty-eight hours of their good-natured jibing about Kylie and a busy night that cut into the previous night's sleep? Ethan shook his head. "I'm heading home to crash."

"Ditto, but a guy has to eat."

"I have stuff to do."

"Gotta clean the house for Kylie, huh? You'll have time to do that and sleep and straighten up your office before she shows up."

"She said not to touch the office. She wants to see it as is."

"That can't be good." Rob gave his head a dire shake. "You're a brave man. I wouldn't want the woman I was interested in seeing my crap."

Liam hooted. "Judging by that photo of them locked together the other night, she's already interested."

Snickers all around. *And here we go again.*

Since the reporter's picture, which had gone viral, the whole crew assumed Ethan and Kylie would become a thing. Ethan wasn't ready for that, and from what Kylie had told him, neither was she. Still, he wouldn't mind revisiting where they'd left off, and fooling around.

"Like I keep saying, the only thing I know for sure is that she's not happy about the photo or the false assumptions people are making." His pointed look included them all.

He headed for the Escalade and noted the slight breeze carrying a hint of fall, a welcome change from the heat.

At home he crashed for a few hours, then cut the grass and bagged the clippings. Stifling the urge to tidy the office, he channeled his energy into cleaning the rest of the house. He sorted through the mail and thought about Kylie and the things he wanted to do with her. Stuff that got him hot and sweaty. But she wasn't coming over for that. Unless she signaled that she wanted the same thing he'd keep his hands to himself.

After a shower and a shave he headed out to buy groceries. Finally, he picked up the mac and cheese at The Rogue, thanking the chef and the rest of the staff with his usual appreciative grin and generous tip.

He put the groceries away and then, whistling and eager to see Kylie, he set the table in the great room. Started to open a bottle of wine, then changed his mind. Tonight was about business, period, and he'd best act like it. Moments after he returned the bottle to the pantry, she arrived.

THE SUN WAS SINKING toward the horizon as Kylie turned onto Ethan's street. He lived in a sprawling, one-story at the far end of a wooded cul-de-sac. The houses she passed were situated some distance from each other among the trees, but for all she knew a busybody like Mrs. Crowley was peering through their window. Which was why Kylie had decided to wear sunglasses and a huge hat, neither of which she needed at this hour.

She rolled down a gravel driveway that had to be at least half a mile long. As she made her way to the front door she kept her head down.

"That's some hat," Ethan commented when he let her in.

She removed it and the sunglasses. "I don't want to take any chances that any of your neighbors might recognize me. How else will the gossip stop?"

"You must've had a rough few days at work."

"Worse than I expected. I tried to follow your advice but it's not so easy to smile and pretend I don't care about that photo. You wouldn't believe the questions and comments, and not just from coworkers. Even people filing accident claims asked about us." She shook her head at the ceiling. "There is no 'us.' "

"I got the same treatment at GLFD. I set everyone straight but they're sure there's more to the story."

If Ethan's closest friends didn't believe him, why would anyone else? There went her appetite.

He directed her to a spacious room split in half by area rugs and furniture. At one end, sleek, modern pieces were arranged comfortably around a fireplace. At the other, a large wood farm table set for two. The entire area had a bright, airy feel, no doubt from the waning sunlight flooding through skylights and the glass sliding doors that opened to a back yard and patio.

"Smell the mac and cheese?" he said. "I'll bet you're hungry. I am."

Kylie wasn't, but the aroma definitely tantalized. Macaroni and cheese had always been her go-to comfort food, and with her stress levels off the charts, she needed comforting. "I can eat any time."

"How about a beer or wine with dinner?"

She wouldn't have minded wine but wanted a clear head when she assessed Ethan's office. "Water is fine. This is what you call a great room, right?"

He nodded. "When I bought the house the living and dining rooms were separate and the place felt cramped, so I knocked out the walls. I'll be back shortly with dinner."

"Can I help?"

"Nah." He gestured at the table. "Relax."

Feeling restless, she wandered around the great room instead. Both area rugs were thick and luxurious, the one in the living room filled with interesting geometric patterns, the one in the dining room a deep red. White walls showcased colorful prints and paintings.

Ethan returned with the food and drinks. They sat down and helped themselves, and he dug in. Kylie managed a few bites but mostly pushed the food around her plate.

"Not hungry after all," he commented.

"I should be—the past few days I haven't eaten much. I don't sleep without waking up in a cold sweat, and when I'm awake I want to throw up."

He frowned. "That second photo has done a bigger number on you than I guessed. And here I wanted to prove that I'm one of the decent guys."

"That's important to you?" Kylie couldn't hide her surprise.

"Hell, yes."

Interesting but puzzling. "You don't have to impress me, Ethan. It's not like we're seeing each other or starting a relationship."

"When my reputation is on the line, your opinion matters. Back to the photo of us. It's nothing like when your ex caused all that trouble, and sure not worth making yourself sick over."

"Tell that to my stomach. I have another skeleton in my closet from a long time ago that I was sure I'd put behind me. But the picture of us kissing dredged up a lot of old feelings, and I realized I haven't." Kylie swallowed.

"Us kissing reminds you of your skeleton? With an opening like that, you have to explain."

"It happened before we moved to Guff's Lake and really isn't worth going into."

"It is if it makes you sick."

Kylie had to agree. "Okay, I'll spare you the details and give you the short version. My parents were never a good fit. Dad has always been a homebody and Mom liked to party, to the point that instead of coming home after work she usually headed for one of the bars in town."

Ethan had stopped eating to listen.

"For as long as I could remember, their marriage was pretty shaky—lots of fighting about alcohol and other men," Kylie said. "In hindsight, it's obvious Mom had a drinking problem. Everything came to a head when I was ten. Dad worked late that day and for once she came straight home from work. As I soon discovered, only to change clothes before a party.

"I didn't want her to go out again but of course she didn't listen to me. By then, Cheryl was used to looking after me and cooking dinner. I guess that's where she learned to mother me."

Kylie rolled her eyes. "For the first time ever, Mom stayed out all night. Which was bad enough, but things got worse when the daily paper ran a picture of her in an intimate dance with her very married boss, a local bigwig."

Ethan whistled. "You're right, that sucks."

"In a town of three thousand people the scandal was huge and sealed the coffin on my parents' dying marriage."

"Did the bigwig's wife divorce him?"

"He was rich and she looked the other way. My mother lost her job and moved to Minneapolis, about a two-hour drive away, but the scandal marched on, along with the rude whispers behind my back and to my face. That's where I learned how cruel kids can be. The pitying looks from teachers made it worse. It wasn't as bad as the Gordon thing, but when you're ten..."

The shame of it all flooded back. Kylie shuddered. "I wanted to hide in my room and never come out. As soon as the attorney filed the divorce papers Dad sold the house and we relocated to Guff's Lake to start fresh. Now you know how I spent my childhood."

"The scars that mark us when we were kids take a long time to shake off." Ethan sounded as if he had a few of his own. "Between your mom and your ex, you've been through a lot. And you're still standing."

"That's something, at least," Kylie agreed.

"It's a lot." He reached across the table and squeezed her hand. She hadn't realized how badly she needed his warm, reassuring touch, and liked it too much for her own good. Managing a small smile, she pulled away.

"Where is your mom now?" he asked.

"We didn't hear from her until she'd joined AA and gotten sober. She apologized to me, Cheryl, and Dad for the pain she caused—step nine in the recovery program. She still lives in Minneapolis. I've seen her once or twice, and now and then we talk on the phone." Ethan seemed grounded and solid, but he'd made that comment about childhood scars. "How did you get rid of your old scars?"

"Determination and grit."

She so admired him. "Tell me your childhood was better than mine."

"It was okay. We didn't have much money. Both my parents held several jobs to keep a roof over our heads. My sister Heather and I took care of ourselves. When we were old enough to work we got jobs and helped with the bills."

"At least you were an intact family."

"True. Eventually, Dad started a house-painting business. He's doing pretty well now. Mom handles the books and works at a florist shop part-time."

"They're still married?"

"Thirty-seven years and counting."

"That's impressive. My dad... He's on his third

marriage and things don't look good. But enough about parents. All this talking has worked up my appetite." Suddenly ravenous, Kylie speared her mac and cheese. It had grown lukewarm but still tasted good. "This is delicious, exactly what I needed."

She was grateful to Ethan for asking about her story and listening while she dumped the family baggage on him. Against her better judgment she was more drawn to him than ever. He seemed like such a great guy, but she was wary and wasn't about to let her defenses down.

"The Rogue's mac and cheese is on my favorites list. I eat it at least once a week." With a gleam in his eyes, he nodded at the last of it. "Wanna split what's left?"

Kylie laughed for the first time in days. "How can I say no? For some reason, when I'm with you I eat a lot. You're a definite appetite stimulant."

"I'll take that as a compliment."

When the meal ended, they cleared the table together. He didn't make any moves on her, thank goodness, even if a part of her wanted him to.

As soon as they cleaned up he led her to his office. All business, then. She heaved an inward sigh of relief.

7

———

Ethan's office contained a sofa and game console as well as the usual desk, file cabinet, and printer. A typical home office—a messy one, with papers stacked on the printer, strewn across the desk, and piled against the wall.

A visible plea for decluttering that got Kylie all fired up. "Thanks for not cleaning up in here."

"I wanted to, but you asked me to leave it as is."

By his gruff tone and the way he scrubbed the back of his neck, allowing her to see the room this way embarrassed him. To his credit, he'd let her in anyway.

Although his discomfort wouldn't help either of them. "Hey, I'm not here to judge—I'm here to help," she assured him.

He nodded and some of the starch went out of his shoulders. And hers.

"Would you mind if I took photos?" she asked. "For when I go home and think about this room."

"As long as you don't blackmail me later."

The humorous glint in his eyes—even better. "I hadn't thought of that, but thanks for the idea," she teased back. "Do you use your desk drawers for filing?"

"Not the way I should."

"Is it okay if I peek in them?"

"It ain't pretty, but go ahead."

"You have a lot of papers in the desk drawers and the rest of your office," she said after she'd glanced through the drawers. "Where do they all come from?"

He looked thoughtful. "Some of it is for my accountant. There are song bits I might use later, contracts for past and future concerts, and other stuff."

"Other stuff?"

"This and that. You know how it goes—toss something and the next day you need it."

He hadn't been kidding when he'd said he needed help. Itching to tackle the job but not wanting to seem too gung-ho, Kylie managed a businesslike nod. "What's in that filing cabinet across the room?"

"It's mostly empty. I'm not much of a filer." He flashed an apologetic smile. "The truth is, for me, filing ranks down there with eating roadkill—I don't do it."

"What if I said it'll make your life easier?"

He looked as if he'd suddenly put a slice of lemon in his mouth.

"You've changed your mind, haven't you?" Kylie so wanted to clean up in here. Oh, well. She did her best to hide her disappointment.

"Hell, no. We both know I need all the help I can get. Most people cringe when they see this room. But you... You light up."

Relieved, she smiled. "I love to organize and I rarely get a chance to do it. Filing isn't so bad if you do it consistently. I'll set up a system that will simplify your life, and teach you how to use it. How does that sound?"

"Okay. I'd like to get this done ASAP. Can you start tomorrow night?"

"Shouldn't you wait for my bid? I don't come cheap. When you see what I charge, you might change your mind."

"I won't—I want you no matter what."

He wasn't all business after all. Maybe. With his hooded gaze, it was hard to tell. All the same, Kylie's sensitive places perked up.

Because, duh—Ethan. Besides being a god physically, feeding her mac and cheese, and letting her tell her story, he wanted to hire her. Talk about a potent and dangerous combination.

On the other hand, he was a publicity magnet and she avoided attention the way she avoided hornets' nests. Then there was the trust issue.

No, no, no.

She cleared her throat. "I'm still going to send you a bid. Watch for it sometime in the next few days."

Pivoting away, she left the room. Ethan followed. "Thanks for feeding me," she said en route to the entry.

"Back at ya for coming over. Hey, do you have a business card?"

As eager as she was to organize his office, she saw no sense in getting ahead of herself. Things could still fall apart, and she didn't want to tempt fate by ordering cards she might never use. "Not yet. Let's see how this pans out."

"Fair enough." He started to open the latch, then paused. "Here we are again, saying good night at the door."

"Different door, different reason."

He glanced at her mouth with the same intent expression as the night of the kiss that had turned her life upside down. Resisting the urge to step closer, put her arms around his neck, and tug him down for another, she instead slung her purse over her shoulder. "I'll send that bid soon."

~

ETHAN WAS in the thick of an erotic dream featuring Kylie when he woke up with a phrase for Rafe and Jillian's song clear in his mind. Hating to miss out on the rest of the dream but needing to capture the words before he forgot them, he grabbed a pen and the notebook stashed on the bedside table in case inspiration struck in the dead of night—desperate times and all that—and scribbled them down.

He read it aloud and almost smiled. Not bad. Figuring more would come, he stayed in bed with his arms tucked behind his head. He thought about Kylie, not the song. Imagined her naked and asleep beside him, her head on the other pillow. He'd wake her with a kiss, then... He got hard.

She turned him on more than any other woman in a long time. Too bad he couldn't get a bead on how she felt. Just when he was sure she was interested, she pulled back. Like when she'd told him about her mom. For a moment there, warmth had shone in her hazel eyes. Then a quick about-face as they cleaned up the dishes and headed to the office. Same thing later, as she was about to leave. He swore she wanted to kiss him again, only she'd left.

He'd lost focus on the lyrics. Muttering, he got up and did his morning thing. With a shower, a bowl of cereal, and a cup of coffee under his belt, he was pumped and determined to create more of the song. Fixing a bad one was easier than staring at a blank page.

The early September morning was sunny but not yet hot. Screw the lyrics—he'd prune dead branches from the honey locust tree out back. As he headed for the glass slider that opened to the patio his cell rang. A local number he didn't recognize. He picked up.

"It's Kylie."

Look at that, the star of his dreams. He broke into a smile. "I was just thinking about you."

"Me?"

"Yeah." Best not mention the dream.

"You're wondering about the bid."

"You said it'd take a few days. Did you finish it last night?"

"No, but I started working on it. Then I realized I didn't have my cell phone. Did I leave it in your office?"

"Hang on—I'll check." He set the pen and notebook down and segued toward the office. There it was, on his desk. "It's here."

"You have no idea how relieved I am."

"You could've phoned me last night or come back and saved yourself the worry."

"I didn't have a way to call, remember? And I didn't realize it was missing until it was too late to go out again."

"Are you at work? I'll bring it to you."

"That'd be great." She gave him the address.

"I know that building from when I did a fire safety inspection there some years back. Ten stories, concrete structure, lots of businesses, with a coffee place and takeout restaurants on the lower level. As I recall, an insurance company fills the entire sixth floor. Is that Coleman's?"

"That's us." She hesitated. "Why don't I meet

you in the parking garage under the building? When you get here call my direct line—the one I'm using now—and I'll come down."

"That's right, you don't want anyone to see me and get the wrong idea about us." An idea Ethan still wanted to explore. "See you soon."

8

Kylie squinted at her office computer screen and tried to focus. Impossible, when any second Ethan would arrive with her phone.

"You're awful quiet," Cricket said as she wandered over from her cubicle. "I'm in dire need of a coffee break. I think I'll wander down to the lobby and buy myself a snack. Can I get you something?"

Flashing a smile, Kylie shook her head. "No, thanks."

As soon as Cricket wandered off Kylie pulled her cosmetics bag from her purse, which she kept locked in the bottom drawer of her desk. She freshened her lipstick and fluffed her hair.

Not long after she relocked the drawer her phone rang. Ethan? Her heart hammered in her chest, which was silly. For goodness' sake, he'd only come to deliver her phone. "Kylie Treadwell," she answered, pleased that she sounded far more relaxed and professional than she felt.

"Hey." His low voice resonated through her. "I'm here, in a fifteen-minute parking slot on the street level of the garage."

"Got it. See you shortly."

In the elevator, she sucked in a deep breath and forced herself to calm down. Exiting a few minutes later, she started toward the short-term parking area, the click of her heels on the concrete floor echoing loudly. Ethan was easy to spot. Buff and sexy in a T-shirt and jeans, leaning against the Escalade with his arms crossed and a bad-boy grin, he was irresistible. Slightly breathless, and not from walking across the garage, she reached him.

His gaze traveled over her. "I like that dress. You look like a businesswoman."

"Which I am."

He got quiet but his eyes kept right on talking, flashing heat and attraction that were impossible to ignore. "Here's your phone."

As he handed her the device she felt the brief warmth of his fingers. A casual touch, yet her legs wobbled. "Thanks," she said, her voice sounding husky to her own ears.

"I dreamed about you last night." He seemed taken aback by his own words. "Forget I said that."

As if. "Was I organizing your office?" He shook his head. "Well, what was I doing?"

"If I told you, you'd slap me."

The way she felt right now she likely wouldn't. She imagined his hands on her and went hot with desire, barely suppressing a moan. Clutching the phone, she cleared her throat. "Thanks for bringing this to me." She intended to step back but somehow moved closer and tugged his head down within easy reach of her lips.

Locking his eyes on hers, he wrapped her close and walked her backward. Dimly, she wondered where they were going. Then forgot everything and lost herself in the most sensual kiss of her life. Slow, deep, probing. He slid his hands through her hair and cupped the back of her head as if he wanted to keep her mouth fused with his.

All too soon he let her go. For an instant she had no idea where she was, but the sound of an approaching vehicle reminded her. She almost leapt from Ethan's arms. The car rolled past.

Had she lost her mind? Throwing herself at him like one of his crazed fans? And in a public garage, where anyone might see. Not the best way to put an end to the gossip.

Now he'd think she was interested in him. She was, but didn't want to be and certainly hadn't wanted him to know. She felt safer that away.

"Take it easy," he said. "There's nothing to worry about. We're in the corner where it's dark."

At least one of them had been thinking

straight. Kylie was grateful and strongly tempted to show her gratitude with another kiss. Reining that urge in, she checked her watch. "I should get back to the office."

His mouth quirked. "You might want to tidy yourself up first."

Avoiding the elevator, she climbed the stairs to the ground floor and ducked into the women's restroom there. Ethan was right—she was a mess. Her hair and lipstick, even her dress was cockeyed. Too bad her comb and cosmetics were in her purse. She did her best, then took the elevator. At least she had her phone back.

By the end of the day Ethan had written half of Rafe and Jillian's song. Not crap, either—decent stuff. Damn, that felt good. Ethan felt good, period, thanks to Kylie. She'd kissed him all on her own, and what a kiss. He wanted a whole lot more.

That evening her bid landed in his email inbox. She didn't come cheap, but she'd warned him. As long as she did a great job, and he had no doubt she would, the price wasn't important. Plus, he'd get to spend more time with her. After he read through the proposal he gave her a call. "I accept your bid."

"Did you even look at it?"

"I read every word." He chuckled.

"It struck you as funny?"

"Not at all. I had a productive day and I'm happy. For weeks, I've been struggling to write the words for a song. Today I made solid progress. That kiss opened things up for me." He lowered his voice." I'm still thinking about it."

She made a sound that could have been a moan of agreement or a groan of misery. "I can't believe I jumped on you like that. I've never... I don't know what came over me."

"I'm your first impulse kiss, huh?" Pleased, he grinned.

"Call it what you will, it's dangerous."

"In a good way. It was definitely hot."

"Don't go getting the wrong idea—it was just a kiss. I'm not at all interested in you."

Could've fooled him. "I'm sure interested in you."

"I didn't know you wrote songs."

She didn't want to talk about what was happening between them. All right. "It's not something I do often, but this is a wedding gift for my crewmate Rafe and his fiancée, Jillian. They're getting married in about a month. The ceremony is for family only at the courthouse. The following weekend they're hosting a big party to celebrate. Mello will play the song at the party, and I'll present them with a recording of it as a keepsake—if I finish in time."

"You have to, Ethan. What a special gift."

"I'm working on it. I've only written half the

song and I still need to compose the music. After that, I'll try it out with the band and get their feedback. Then we'll record it. All that takes awhile."

"You'll get it done."

"I appreciate the vote of confidence. Back to organizing my office. How about Saturday?"

"You weren't kidding when you said ASAP."

"I want to get this done and put it behind me. The sooner you start, the sooner you finish."

"Hold on there. This isn't a solo endeavor. You'll be involved every step of the way."

"Oh, man," he grumbled. "Why didn't I know that?"

"I assumed you did. Next time, if there is one, I'll make sure to tell the customer."

"I would."

"If you want to back out..."

That she thought he might change his mind bothered him. "I said I'd do this. I'm in."

"Even if you have a homework assignment before we start?"

Not that, too. "Lay it on me."

"I want you to go through all your papers and throw away what you don't need."

"Like I said the other night, I don't know what I'll need in the future."

"Get rid of what you can."

The remains of his good mood evaporated. "Gee, that sounds easy."

"If throwing the hard copies away makes you

nervous, scan the documents and store them in a file on your hard drive. You can also make an 'un-decided' pile and we'll winnow it down together. Meanwhile, I'll set up an easy-to-use online spreadsheet that will help you manage your data. We're going to need time to organize and transfer the information to your spreadsheet."

"Okay." He grimaced. "How much time will all this take?"

"That depends on how much help you need with those papers. We could finish in one day or four or five."

The thought of sorting and organizing for days on end filled him with dread. "Can't say I'm excited about this project dragging on."

"Believe me, when you get it done you'll feel much better. Once you sort through everything, we'll schedule a date for the job."

"I'll be ready Saturday."

"But tomorrow's Friday. That's not much time."

"No problem—I'll start tonight."

"Are you sure? You have a lot of papers."

If that wasn't a challenge... "You don't think I can do it?"

"You tell me."

"I've made up my mind and that's that."

"You're either determined or delusional."

"A little of both." She laughed, a pretty sound, and he grinned despite himself. "Look at you, already figuring me out."

"I had no idea I was that bright. There is one more small task. You need hanging files for your desk and filing cabinet. Get them in assorted colors."

"I won't have time to get them and finish the sorting. Will you pick them up for me? I'll pay you for your time."

"It's your money."

"See you Saturday." Ethan disconnected. Squaring his shoulders, he headed to his office.

9

Dressed in cutoffs and an old top for a day of hard work, and determined not to think about kissing Ethan because she definitely wasn't going to indulge in any more of that, Kylie knocked at his door.

"Morning," he said. "You're right on time."

"I try." No man had the right to look that sexy in a loose T-shirt and faded jeans. But then, he'd probably look sexy in a clown suit, damn him.

Inside, she handed him the bag of supplies she'd bought. "Here are the file folders. Are you ready to get started?"

"Sure am." He yawned.

Up close, she noted his slightly bloodshot eyes and the circles underneath. "Late night?"

"Two in a row. Sorting through my papers took longer than I estimated. I'm going to need a lot of coffee today. You, on the other hand, seem disgustingly lively. Is that a 'told you so' gloat?"

"When you obviously put in so much time

and effort? I wouldn't dare. My energy comes from pure excitement for the job ahead."

"You're going to need it." He scrubbed his hand over his face. "Before we dig into this, I need more caffeine. You?"

"Yes please, with a splash of milk."

"I'll meet you in the office."

Not sure what to expect, Kylie went into the room. Four bulging trash bags had replaced the stacks of paper against the wall, and scattered papers and confetti from the shredder littered the carpet. Still a mess, but definite progress.

Itching to get to work, she collected the papers off the floor. One, a square of hot pink, caught her eye. She smelled the cloying perfume even before she picked it up. Wrinkling her nose, she read the message.

"Tami" with a heart over the "i" had written her name and phone number, along with a promise of an unforgettable night. The note ended with a lipstick imprint of pouty lips.

It shouldn't have bothered Kylie but did.

Ethan appeared with two steaming mugs. "What've you got there?" he asked.

"Something I found on the floor. I wasn't going to read it but couldn't help myself." She handed it to him.

Glancing at it, he shrugged. "I don't remember the woman or the note."

"But you saved it."

"No idea why. I usually toss that stuff as soon

as I get it." Crumpling the note into a ball, he lobbed it into the nearly full wastebasket.

He didn't seem at all concerned or interested in Tami, whoever she was. But it was a good reminder for Kylie to watch herself.

She pulled the folders and hanging files from the office supply bag. "We'll use the hanging files to organize the folders into groups—for example, a hanging file called 'Insurance' containing folders for home insurance, car insurance, and so on. That way you'll be able to quickly find a document when you need it. If you get into the habit of either scanning or filing papers as soon as you get them, and adding the info to your online spreadsheet, you'll simplify your life."

"If you say so. Why are the hanging files in different colors?"

"Color-coded categories will make your life easier. Green for financials and contracts, blue for insurance, red for bills, and so on." She frowned at him. "Your eyes are glazing over, but once we get started the system will make more sense."

Several hours later, Kylie's empty stomach complained with a hungry growl.

Ethan's lips quirked. "Must be lunchtime."

Arching her back to stretch the muscles, she nodded. "We both need a break."

As she reached for her purse he arched his eyebrows. "Going somewhere?"

"No, I put my sandwich in here—a PB&J."

"Save that for another time. I make a mean grilled cheese."

"You fed me the other night. If you count the Hearthstone, that's twice—enough for one man."

"Hey, you're stuck here all day with this." He gestured at the mess.

"May I remind you, you're paying a lot for my services."

"You'll make it up to me."

"How?"

An irresistible smile lit his whole face and set off tiny sparks inside. "I'll think of something. Come into the kitchen while I make the sandwiches."

"Only if I get to help."

He let her take the plates from the cabinet and open the bread, then pointed at a barstool. "Sit. You deserve it."

What man had ever said anything that sweet? She melted a little. "If you insist."

Perched on the stool, she watched him wash up and dry his hands on a towel. Not an exciting activity, but with his biceps contracting and flexing and his tee hugging his shoulders and outlining his lean belly...

"You're checking me out—and you said you weren't interested." This time, a cocky grin that brought heat to her cheeks. "You're cute when you blush."

While the sandwiches cooked on the stove,

he wandered over and rotated the stool so that she faced him. "Stand up."

"What for?" she said, rising all the same.

"It's my turn to kiss you."

He tipped her chin up. Her mind warned her to stop him but her body didn't listen. Oh, what a kiss. One wasn't enough. The repeat was even better, with tongue and a lot of passion. Eat your heart out, Lipstick Tami!

Forget lunch. Forget that Ethan enjoyed playing the field and relished attention from adoring women all over town. Kylie didn't want to marry the guy, but she wanted this for as long as it lasted. She wriggled in closer.

The smell of something burning distracted her. Her eyes flew open and Ethan jerked back.

"The grilled cheese," they cried at the same time.

Moving faster that a man his size had any right to, he rescued the sandwiches. "I hate to toss these," he said.

"Then don't. Show me where you keep the table knives and I'll scrape off the blackened parts."

"Never thought I'd almost ruin our lunch," he said while she scraped away. "You distract me no end."

She couldn't stop a smile.

"Oh, you like that, do you?"

"As a matter of fact..." She crooked her finger at him. "One more time."

·"Vixen." He kissed her again—once before he pulled away. "Let's eat before these get cold."

LATE IN THE AFTERNOON, Ethan settled his hands low on his hips and took stock of the hard copy documents he'd elected to keep. There were a fair amount, enough to cover the entire dining room table, but at least they were organized. More or less. "That's a chore I never want to do again."

"Use the new system consistently and you won't have to," Kylie said. "You're not quite done yet, but you deserve a pat on the back for what you accomplished." She yawned.

She looked as beat as he felt. A yawn of his own followed. "Those things are contagious. I don't care how close we are to being done, I can't take anymore."

She checked her watch and her eyes widened. "No wonder. Not counting lunch, we've been at this for seven hours. Two people can only do so much in one day."

"Amen. I don't have any problem working forty-eight hours straight at the station. But this..." He pantomimed sticking his finger down his throat.

As he'd anticipated, she smiled. "Very funny, Mr. Goldberg. If we quit now, I won't be able to upload the spreadsheet I made for you or show you how to use it. You won't be able to use your dining room table either. Is that going to be a problem?"

He shook his head. "The spreadsheet can wait and I'll eat in the kitchen or in front of the tube."

"All right then, that's it for today. When do you want to finish up?"

"How much longer do you think it'll take?" He moved to his favorite armchair, sat down, and swiveled to face her.

"Not long if you label the folders and transfer the documents into them yourself. Hours if you wait for me and we do it together. You decide." She checked out his seat. "That chair is so cool."

"It's also a rocker." He demonstrated. "Right now, I'm in no shape to think about either choice. All I know is, I want to get this done. Tomorrow works for me."

"I can't. Cheryl's husband is at some weekend work thing and I'm spending the day with her and my nephew Lucas. She's making brunch."

Kylie licked her lips and Ethan chuckled. God, he loved hanging out with her. "What's she serving?"

"Who cares? Whatever she makes will be out of this world."

"That good, huh?"

"She was born with the cooking gene. Food, the soaps she sells—which are top-quality, by the way—if she makes it, it turns out great."

"You don't cook?"

"Not unless I have to."

"What's your special gene?"

She gave him a "You need to ask?" look. "Organizing. I'm available after dinner Wednesday."

"That's a long time to go without seeing you."

She rolled her eyes. "I'll bet you say that to all the girls."

"Only when I mean it." Over the course of the day she'd changed, giving him lip laced with humor and openly eager to kiss him. He liked this side of her a lot. "Come over here and try out this chair."

"When you're still in it? Move, big guy." She caught hold of his hands and attempted to pull him up. He let her pull on his arms but didn't move.

"It's more fun with two." Tugging her onto his lap, he wrapped his arms around her from behind. "Am I right?"

"What am I, three years old?"

"With that body?" Unable to resist, he shifted her around and kissed her. "I sure enjoy doing that."

"So I noticed. If you want to do it again..."

"Oh, I do."

Things got a little crazy, the chair tipping and bobbing as they tried to get comfortable. "To hell with this." Lifting her in his arms, he moved to the sectional. "Much better. Now, where were we?"

"Here, I think." She placed his hands on her breasts.

"I wasn't there yet."

"You wanted to be."

And how. "One of these days, that sassy mouth of yours is going to land you in big trouble."

"Sassy? I—"

He thumbed her nipples and she broke off. Her breathing ragged, she tilted her head back and thrust into his palms.

He slid his hands under her shirt and inside her bra. Before long, she was restless and gasping sounds of pleasure. Beautiful and sexy. *His.* He wanted her, but things were getting too hot, too soon. Another deep kiss, then he tore his mouth from hers. "That was even more fun than the swivel chair."

"You're such a guy."

She smoothed her shirt into place. Her face was flushed, her lips pinker than usual, and her hair loose and wild. To say he was aroused was an understatement, but he managed to stand and walk her to the door.

"Thanks for today," he said. "You did a fantastic job."

"With your help. As tired as I am, I enjoyed it."

"Me, too. All of it."

"Even sorting all those papers?" she asked.

"Not that so much, but everything else." He

locked eyes with her, and it was all he could do not to start up with her again.

"See you next week," she said, and slipped out the door.

10

Even before Kylie peered through Cheryl's screen door Sunday morning, the aroma of freshly baked orange date muffins tickled her nostrils. Her mouth watered like a Pavlovian dog's. "I'm here," she called out.

Four-year-old Lucas, his big eyes and mop of curls guaranteed to someday drive girls wild, beamed and let her in. "Hi, Aunt Kylie!"

"Hiya, big guy." He wasn't keen on hugs and kisses, so she ruffled his hair. And noted the streak of what looked like dough on his cheek. "Have you been helping your mama with the baking?"

He nodded and puffed up with importance. "I put the orange juice in and turned on the mixer. And I got to lick the bowl."

"Lucky you."

They headed for the kitchen, where Kylie greeted her sister with a hug. "Your house always smells so good—especially in here."

"Lucas and I have been cooking up a storm. Coffee's ready."

Kylie helped herself, humming as she added milk and stirred. She licked the spoon, then set it down.

Cheryl studied her with a quizzical look. "You seem unusually happy this morning."

High spirits and heart-singing excitement had kept her up late the night before and awakened her early this morning. She should've been tired but wasn't. "I get to have brunch with you and Lucas."

"That's great, but you're almost glowing."

"Am I?" Kylie smiled. Decluttering and organizing, and getting paid for it—how cool was that? Thanks to Ethan's support and encouragement, she was beginning to visualize Clutter Buster as a real business. Add in all those delicious kisses and the day couldn't have been better.

"Hmm. Were you with—" Kylie's sister glanced at her son—"Ethan last night?"

"No, but we spent a big chunk of the day together."

"I need to hear about this *now*. Lucas honey, why don't you play with your Legos until brunch is ready?"

As soon as the little guy scampered off, Cheryl eyed her. "Tell me."

"I was at his house."

"That's quick. Just call me matchmaker." Kylie's sister polished her nails on her apron.

"It's not what you think. Well, a little of that. Most of the time we—"

"Go back. A little of what?"

"Kissing. Actually, we made out." Cheryl broke into a huge smile, and so did Kylie. Bursting to talk about Clutter Buster, she went on. "Don't get me wrong, we spent the majority of the day cleaning his office. Which was a mess and still is, but we're getting there. And he's paying me." Unable to contain herself, she hugged herself and squealed.

Cheryl's jaw dropped in shock. "Let me get this straight—Ethan is paying you money to clean and he also made out with you? That sounds a little kinky. You're no one's maid."

"Jump to conclusions, why don't you. This isn't about vacuuming and dusting, it's about getting rid of the clutter in his office and organizing the rest. Most people, Ethan included, have no idea how to do it or where to start. When he found out I'm into that, he hired me. It's a dream come true!"

"You've always been an organizer. You did it with your closet, and I remember when you set up the kitchen for Dad after we moved to Guff's Lake. Now you're doing that for other people? Why don't I know about this?"

Cheryl didn't hide her hurt feelings, and Kylie suffered a pang of guilt. But only for a moment.

"You're always mothering me and I was afraid if I told you, you'd nag me to start a real business when I'm not sure I want to."

"I don't mother you."

"You so do."

"Only because I want you to be happy."

"I know, and I appreciate that. To be honest, I wasn't ready to talk about my pie-in-the-sky idea until now. Testing my skills at Ethan's changed everything. I had a ball and I'm super psyched."

"Are you sure you're not confusing the work with the man?"

"Not at all. Transforming a misused space into something that makes the lives of the people using that space better? I love doing that."

"I haven't seen you this exhilarated in forever. You almost sound like a cleaning and organizing evangelist."

"That's exactly what I am."

"This is your bliss! I don't understand it, but who cares? You can't not open this business." Cheryl rubbed her hands together. "We'll be small-business owners together."

"Not so fast. This is why I didn't tell you before. I'm not ready to make a decision yet."

"Why not?"

"Because starting Clutter Buster would be risky."

"Great name. The risk will be minimal if you keep your day job and ease into the business bit by bit, like I did. It'll mean late nights and busy weekends, but your enthusiasm will carry you."

"You sound an awful lot like Ethan."

Cheryl grinned. "I like him more and more, even if we haven't been introduced."

As did Kylie, but she refused to let her feelings go any deeper than they were. Down that road lay heartache. Because face it, sooner or later, whatever this thing between them was would come to an end. Ethan was happy with his life as a single man. He'd said so. Regardless, she intended to enjoy it while it lasted. "Don't get your hopes up," she warned. "He's an amazing guy and I'm having fun. But I don't expect anything to come of this."

"Ah, now I understand. You're protecting yourself. The important thing is, you're back in the game. Hurray! But don't you think—hold on, while I finish up here."

Cheryl lifted the lid of a large pan and sprinkled cheese over what smelled like the best frittata ever. Sensing unasked-for and unwanted advice on the horizon, Kylie set her mug down. "Smells like breakfast is almost ready. I'll go get Lucas."

~

"HELL OF A FIRE," Liam commented as Ethan, Rafe, and Tony climbed aboard the fire truck in the early evening. "And you two," he said, nodding at Ethan and Rafe. "Unbelievable."

Ethan was still in shock. A wall fan in a fourth-floor apartment of a four-story building had shorted out and started the fire. The renters were out and the fire quickly spread. By the time the crew arrived, flames and smoke had consumed a large part of the hallway on the fourth floor. A couple trapped there, frantic to get their children to safety, dropped their three-year-old son from their balcony. Rafe caught him. Ethan was a quarter of the way up a ladder when their infant daughter followed, straight into his arms.

Minutes later, Liam and Tony had successfully rescued the parents while other team members guided stranded tenants to safety.

"The entire crew did great," Ethan said. "Thanks to our rapid response, no one was seriously hurt." He noted Rafe's pinched expression. Under the soot and dirt his face was likely gray with pain. "Except maybe you. How's your back?"

"After a couple aspirin and the usual ice and heat treatments tonight, I'll be as good as new."

Ethan wasn't convinced. The boy Rafe had caught must have weighed close to forty pounds. "You'd better be—you're getting married in two weeks."

"If I have to, I'll take it easy next week." Rafe narrowed his eyes at Ethan. "The way you're favoring your right arm, you're hurting too."

"I pulled a muscle in my biceps. I'll live."

"A massage might help," Tony suggested.

"Can you recommend someone?"

"Kylie's coming over tomorrow night, right?" Liam winked. "I'm sure she'd love to help you out."

Ethan approved of the idea. "But I can hear the conversation: 'Hey, Kylie, forget the office and massage my arm instead.' That'd go over big. I'll follow Rafe's plan—pain reliever, heat, and ice. By the time she shows up, I should be almost back to normal."

11

When Ethan and several of his crewmates stepped outside to enjoy the evening after dinner, he pulled out his phone and called Kylie.

"Hi," she said, sounding surprised to hear from him. "Are you calling to reschedule tomorrow night?"

"No. My sister Heather—"

"Tell her about your arm," Rob interrupted.

Ethan glared at him. "Shut it. Anyway, Heather—"

"Give me that phone." Rob grabbed the thing from Ethan's unsuspecting grasp. "Hi, Kylie, this is Rob, one of Ethan's better-looking teammates. He messed up his arm pretty bad and he could use a massa—"

Ethan snatched his phone back and moved away. "Don't pay any attention to him."

"What happened to your arm?"

"I'll get to that. First, let me tell you why I called."

"Let me guess—you want to get a jump on tomorrow night and are looking for guidance on putting those folders together."

"Hell, no. My sister and her husband stopped by Sunday. They saw the folders and the papers on the dining room table, and the questions started."

"You were working on your filing? That makes me happy."

"I plied myself with beer and chips and got about halfway done before I clocked in here yesterday. I told Heather and Mike what you're doing for me. One thing led to another. Now she wants to hire you."

"Really?" She packed all kinds of pleased surprise into that one word. "That's so cool. Does their home office look like yours?"

"They don't have one. Heather's impressed that you persuaded me to get rid of old papers and organize the rest. She thinks I have packrat tendencies because we grew up poor."

"I don't think so. Otherwise, the rest of your house would look more like your office. Your problem is, you don't know what to do with your papers. Once I put your filing system in place, that will change."

"Time will tell."

"Hearing that makes my clutter buster heart shrink in dread."

He chuckled. "To be on the safe side, I'll put you on a retainer."

"There's an idea I hadn't thought of. Tell me you won't let yourself slip backward."

"After all this hard work? I won't. If I didn't want to change I wouldn't have hired you. I'm stoked to finish this project. And to see you," he added in a low voice for her ears only. "Tomorrow night can't come soon enough." The catch in her breath reminded him of the other night. The things he wanted to do with her... He started to get aroused, but this wasn't the time or place. "I gave Heather your number. You should hear from her soon."

"Wonderful. What does she want to work on?"

"She didn't say, but after she and Mike got married a year or so ago they bought a house. They still haven't unpacked all the boxes."

"I'm sure I'll find out when she calls. What's wrong with your arm?"

"Nothing much. I pulled a muscle."

"I did that to my hamstring once. It hurt."

"This happened at a fire today."

"Are injuries a regular thing for firefighters?"

"Not if we can help it. Today was a little out of the ordinary." He told her about the fast-moving fire and catching the baby.

"That sounds dangerous."

"Part of the job. Anyway, it screwed up my arm."

"I would've been scared of dropping her."

"There was no time to worry about that. I didn't think about what could have happened until later." He swallowed hard. "I'm awful glad I didn't miss."

"Me, too. I'm in awe."

Her soft voice wrapped around him. He closed his eyes and imagined her fingers soothing his sore arm and stroking another suddenly swollen body part.

"Ethan? Are you still there?"

"Yeah. Rafe had it worse. He caught the same couple's three-year-old, who weighed double the baby, and messed up his back."

"Poor guy."

"The important thing is, both kids are okay and so are their parents. The local news channels probably ran a clip of us tonight."

"Shoot, I missed that. I'll look for it online."

"Everyone in the building survived," Ethan went on. "Pretty amazing when you see the damage."

He shuddered. As much as he loved firefighting, the work wasn't easy.

"What if another call comes in tonight? Will you be able to use your arm?"

"If I have to. It wouldn't be the first time. When the adrenaline pumps through my veins the pain fades."

"You really are a hero."

"I couldn't do anything without the rest of the crew. We're a team—we have each others' backs."

"You're a lucky man."

Didn't he know it.

"Tomorrow night, I'll kiss that owie and make it all better," she said.

He already felt better for talking to her. Leaning against the siding of the building, he smiled. "Promise?"

SECONDS AFTER ETHAN let Kylie in and shut the door, he kissed her. She melted into his warmth and let her purse and the Guff's Lake Books bag she'd brought slip from her fingers.

"It's good to see you," he said when he let her go.

"You, too." Tingling everywhere, she collected her things. "I saw footage of the fire online. You didn't mention standing on a ladder when you caught the baby. That was unbelievable."

"As I said, it's part of the job."

He didn't seem to realize what a hero he was, took what he'd done in stride as if it were no big deal. Her admiration and respect for him grew to new heights.

"What's in there?" he said, eyeing the bag as he picked it up. "Let me guess—a book that lays out the filing system you want me to use."

The look of distaste on his face was priceless. Fighting a smile—playing along was such fun—

she sighed with mock gravity. "Something like that. See for yourself."

"Shoot me now," he muttered as he pulled the paperback out. "The bookstore must've put the wrong book in your bag. This is one of Dave Barry's. He's funny."

"He always makes me laugh, and you know what the experts say about laughter."

"Organizing my office is a pain in the ass, but I'm not that bad off."

"No, but between the filing you did the other day and what we'll be doing tonight, you could use a giggle. You also had a rough day yesterday, and your arm..."

She hadn't noticed the ugly bruise on the inside of his biceps until now. Dark purple and tinged with red, it spanned the crook of his arm. She winced. "That looks more serious than a pulled muscle."

"The muscle injury is on the other arm, and feels better today. I got the bruise when I gripped the ladder to catch the baby."

Kylie hurt for him. "It looks painful. Why didn't you say something? We could've postponed."

"Miss seeing you? No way. I like my present. Come here, so I can thank you properly."

This kiss made her want to forget about his office and everything but the two of them for a few hours. But she had a job to do, a job that excited her. Reluctantly, she stepped from his arms. "Shall we get to work?"

"Don't I get my owies kissed first? You promised."

Stifling a laugh, she shook her finger at him. "Not till you label the rest of those folders. Then you have to group them, and then..."

"Stop already. I get the message."

"Do you want help?" He shook his head. "While you work on that, I'll go into your office and load the spreadsheet onto your laptop. I'll check on you in a little while."

"How's it going?" she asked when she ventured toward the dining room table sometime later.

"Almost finished." He patted the chair next to him. "Sit and keep me company."

"Heather called this afternoon," Kylie said as he worked. "I'm going over there Saturday to take a look at the master bedroom."

"Good to know. All done."

"Great. Let's move the folders to the office and tackle the hanging files."

It didn't take long to place the folders in their respective hanging files. Kylie opened the spreadsheet and explained how to use it with the filing system. "Does this makes sense to you?"

Ethan nodded. "Filing on a regular basis seems a lot easier than I guessed, and the spreadsheet helps. I can do this."

"Imagine that," she teased, and gave herself

mental props for a job well done. "Would you mind if I borrow that quote? I don't have to use your name."

"Uh, okay. What for?"

"I think it'll sound great on a business card."

"Then you decided to open Clutter Buster?"

"I wasn't sure until this minute, but yes."

"Atta girl."

His smile felt like a burst of sunshine. Having a man not only interested in her but encouraging her to follow her dreams was a brand-new experience. She could fall for him so easily. Thank goodness she was smart enough not to let that happen.

12

Decluttering and filing behind him at last, Ethan stood in the doorway beside Kylie and surveyed his much tidier office. "Never thought I'd say this, but the end product is worth all that hard work."

She cupped her ear. "Would you mind repeating that?"

"Beat it over my head, why don't you?" he teased. "You were right."

She beamed at him. "Get rid of those trash bags and give the room a good vacuuming, and you're ready to go."

"May as well do that now." His muscles protesting, he grimaced and hefted two of the overflowing bags in each hand.

Kylie's smiled faded. "I forgot about your arms. Give me two of those. Then I'll vacuum."

With the exception of Heather years ago, no one had ever taken care of him. He wasn't about to let Kylie. "I'm good."

"What you are is stubborn. All right, you take the trash and I'll clean the carpet. Where do you store the vacuum?"

He started to object, but she put her hands on her hips. "Do you want me to kiss that sore arm or not?"

"You drive a tough bargain. The utility room is behind the kitchen."

When he returned to the office after dumping the trash, the roar of the vacuum filled the room. Nothing sexy about a woman in old jeans and a loose T-shirt pushing a machine around—except when she leaned forward to clean under his desk. The denim hugged her behind, driving him all kinds of crazy.

She shut it off and blew the hair out of her eyes. "There. Time for an 'after' shot to go with the 'before' photo I took. I'm texting both to you now."

Barely able to think for wanting her, he pointed at the arm with the pulled muscle. "I'm still waiting for that kiss."

Kylie huffed out a breath, her phony exasperation ruined by the twinkle in her eyes. "If I must."

"Both arms?"

"You're incorrigible. Would you rather stand here or sit?"

His preference was to lie down with her, but he didn't want to push his luck. "Sit on the sectional."

"All right, for a little while. Then I have to go. My day starts extra early tomorrow."

"We have early morning meetings at the station, too," he told her as they headed for the living room.

"This isn't a meeting, it's an appointment at an auto body shop. I get to inspect a minivan involved in a fender bender."

He sat down, then nodded at the space beside him. "That's cool."

"I wouldn't go that far, but it does get me out of my cubicle. Also, there's a really good bakery down the street with the best chocolate mint cupcakes."

"A definite perk." He stretched out his arm. "Do the bruise first."

"Are you sure? I don't want to hurt you."

"I'll let you know."

She pressed her lips softly to his skin, the touch as light as a butterfly's wings. "How was that?"

Sweet and hot at the same time. "Soothing. Now, the other arm."

"Show me where the pulled muscle is," she said when she'd switched sides.

He gestured along his inner biceps.

"On the inside of this arm, too? I wish I could really make it better." She kissed the area and his body went hard. "Right there?"

He shifted his weight. "Trust me, this helps. Up and over a little."

"Right here?"

"That's good, but..." He pointed at his mouth.

"You didn't pull a face muscle."

"Can't blame a guy for trying." Using his finger, he raised her chin. "My turn to kiss you."

He knew by the tilt of her lips that she was about to give him some sass. As tempted as he was to hear it, he had other things on his mind. He brushed his mouth across hers, slow and teasing.

Wrapping her arms around his neck, she met him kiss for kiss until they were both breathing hard. He helped her out of her T-shirt, then reached to remove his own. He'd worn a shirt that buttoned up the front to avoid causing himself pain, but his arms still hurt. He winced.

"Let me." On her knees, Kylie unbuttoned the shirt and eased it off. "There."

"What would I do without you, Nurse Kylie?" She was still on her knees, her lace bra too tempting to ignore. Anchoring her where she was, he caught her nipple gently in his teeth.

She gripped his shoulders. "Too hard?" he asked.

"I'm not sure. Maybe you should try that without my bra. On both breasts."

The bra disappeared and they were face to face, both naked from the waist up. "You're beautiful," he said.

"You're not bad, either." She ran her finger

down the faint scar on his chest. "What happened there?"

"Second-degree burn, a memento from my rookie days."

"I'll kiss that one, too."

She moved her mouth along his skin. Climbed onto his lap and straddled him, her soft parts cradling his hard-on, her shifting and squirming teaching him what drove her wild.

Torture and pleasure and not enough. Wanting more, he reached for the button on her jeans.

"Don't," she said, placing her hand on his.

He nodded and put her off his lap. With her back to him, Kylie rescued her bra and tee from the floor. While she put them on, Ethan struggled into his shirt.

Fully dressed, she turned toward him. "Thanks for stopping when I asked you to. You really are one of the good guys."

At last, she saw him as a good guy. Great, but Ethan was more interested in the rest of what she'd said. If her ex or some other man had hurt her physically... His hands curled into fists. "Is that unusual for you?" he asked, keeping his tone deceptively mild.

"I've never been forced, but in my experience men either try to coax me into having sex or accuse me of being a tease. I don't like it, but I understand. After all, they are male."

"No one deserves a pass for being an ass. When you're with me you don't have to worry. No matter how badly I want you, I'll wait until you're ready."

She gave him a long, measuring look, as if she didn't quite buy that. Sucking in a breath—her opinion still mattered a great deal—he looked her square in the eyes.

When she finally nodded, he exhaled in relief. "FYI, the band is heading up to Portland Saturday for a concert," he said before she left. "I'll be in touch when I get back on Sunday. Good luck with my sister."

He kissed her one last time, a sweet taste to hold him until he saw her again, then watched from the doorway until her car disappeared in the darkness.

~

FROM THE START, Kylie liked Ethan's sister. Shorter and rounder than Kylie, with curly red hair and warm blue eyes, she looked nothing like her brother. But her friendly smile was equally infectious.

"Welcome to our home," she said with a natural warmth that made Kylie feel comfortable.

"I'm excited to be here."

"Ethan said you would be. This is my husband, Mike."

The big teddy bear of a man beside Heather

shook Kylie's hand. "Good to meet you. You come highly recommended."

Something else to thank Ethan for. Kylie planned several ways to convey her gratitude, all of them centered around sex. Which she'd been thinking about since she'd left his house the other night. After three years without sex she was more than ready. Why not with Ethan? She knew where he stood and had no problems with that.

"We just got a new toy—an espresso maker—and we like showing it off," Mike said. "Can I make you a coffee?"

Between excitement and a cup at home, Kylie was already caffeinated enough. "Maybe later?"

He looked disappointed. "Another time."

After a few more minutes of chitchat, Heather eyed him. "Don't you want to go to the hardware store before you meet your friends at the bowling alley?"

"Right—you want me out of your hair. See you later, hon." He kissed her and left.

When the door shut behind him, Heather lowered her voice. "I love that man, but I'm glad he's gone. Now we can get some work done. Let me show you the bedroom. The boxes I mentioned are in the closet. I'd like to empty them, but I have no idea where to put the contents."

"That's what I'm here for—to help."

As she had at Ethan's office, Kylie spent a fair amount of time poking around, snapping photos, taking notes, and mentally rubbing her hands together. She could hardly wait to get started. "I can do wonders for this room," she said later. "And your closet."

"I was hoping you'd say that. What's the next step?"

"I'll email you a bid by the end of the week." With any luck, Heather and Mike would accept it. "Meanwhile, you should go through those boxes and decide what you want near at hand, what you're comfortable storing, and what to get rid of."

"I've been thinking about doing that for ages. Guess I needed a gentle push from you." Heather smiled.

Kylie smiled back. "You're a lot more open to suggestions than your brother was."

"Ethan has always been hard-headed. I'm dying to know how you convinced him to clean up his office. You can tell me over an espresso. You ought to try one. My favorite is chocolate."

"Chocolate espresso?" Kylie licked her lips. "How can I say no?"

"A kindred spirit—I knew it." Heather worked the espresso machine in the small kitchen. They took their coffees to the table in a sunny nook facing the back yard. "Dish on my brother."

"There isn't much to say. I mentioned Clutter Buster the night he took me to the Hearthstone for dinner, but I hadn't started the business. The following week I stopped by to look at his office, the same as I did your bedroom this morning. He hired me. He's my first client. If you hire me, you'll be the second. This espresso is wonderful."

"Mike and I love it. I see what Ethan meant about your enthusiasm for cleaning and organizing. It really is contagious."

"I'm weird that way."

"You and my brother have a thing going on, huh?"

Where in the world had she come up with that? "He's a great guy, but I wouldn't go that far."

"It's a thing, all right. The expression on his face when he talks about you, and yours now are dead giveaways. And that romantic photo of you two in the paper..." Heather sighed. "As far as I know, you're the first woman he's kissed at the end of a fundraiser date. And the last, now that he's given up volunteering."

Kylie made a face. "Don't remind me. I hate publicity."

"Oh? Most women would love to show off a photo of themselves in my brother's arms. Still, after what happened last year, I was surprised that he kissed you. You must've wowed him."

Heather had that backward—*Ethan* had wowed *Kylie*. "What happened last year?"

"He didn't tell you? The woman who won the date decided she was his girlfriend. For weeks, she drove him nuts, showing up where she wasn't invited, calling the station and dropping in.... A real nutcase."

"No way. What happened?"

"Ethan told her the truth, that he wasn't interested. Whenever she showed up, he said it again and told her to leave. After almost a month of that she finally got the message and moved on." Heather shook her had. "My brother and women... You wouldn't believe what some of them do to get his attention. You'd never know from looking at him today that in high school, girls wanted nothing to do with him. He was a total dork."

"He mentioned being scrawny. That doesn't make him a dork."

"Believe me, he was. And it made his life miserable. He was bullied and picked on something awful."

Kylie had had no idea.

"I was plenty upset, but I couldn't do much about it," Heather went on. "His guy friends were social misfits like him and no help at all, and forget girls."

"The principal and your parents didn't step in?"

"Ethan didn't tell the principal, and our parents were always working and didn't have time for much else." Heather shook her head. "He wouldn't have told them anyway. He wanted to handle it himself, the same as he did his stalker. Told you he's hard-headed."

Kylie's heart went out to the boy Ethan had been. She'd had her share of problems with the scandal that had pushed her mother out of town and her father's marriages and divorces, but she'd never been bullied. "How does a high school kid cope on his own with something like that?"

"I can only speak for Ethan. He never showed fear, even when they beat him up."

Kylie shuddered. "Surely someone noticed the bruises."

"Most of the blows were where they didn't show. But that's all behind him. Today, he's a big, buff, popular guy, with two great careers and plenty of friends. Now there's you."

"We like each other well enough, but don't go getting the wrong idea," Kylie said, just as she'd told Cheryl. "Your brother isn't ready for serious."

Heather gave her a speculative look. "Mike used to say the same thing. Then I came along." She glanced at her wedding ring and smiled. "If it happened for me and Mike, it could happen for you and Ethan."

The one thing Kylie knew with certainty was that she and Ethan shared a strong, mutual physical attraction. Other than that, they really had nothing in common. "Or not."

13

As soon as Ethan returned home from Portland, he dropped off his band members, grabbed a quick burger for lunch, then headed straight for Kylie's. He needed to go home and get some things done before his double shift tomorrow, but he hadn't received the bill for his office reorganization and needed to settle up. More than that, he wanted to see her. Wanted her, period.

He pulled up at the duplex. Her car was in the carport and the front door was open, no doubt to take advantage of the fresh September air. In the other half of the building, a woman with gray hair and oversize glasses was trimming plants in her small front yard. She glanced at him. He nodded hello and continued up Kylie's walkway.

The pruning shears dropped from the neighbor's hand. "Ethan Goldberg—you came back!"

He tried to place her and couldn't. "Have we met?"

"Not personally, but I feel as if I know you. I'm May Crowley."

Nothing he hadn't heard before, both from Mello fans and people who owned a calendar. He pasted on the public smile he'd perfected. "Good to meet you, Mrs. Crowley."

"You as well." She beamed at him. " Kylie will be thrilled to see you again." Cupping her hands around her mouth, she called out in a singsong voice, "Kylie, someone's here to see you."

An instant later, Kylie's screen door opened and she stepped onto her front stoop.

"Look who came calling," the older woman cooed. "This time, he's not leaving without autographing my calendar. Stay where you are, Ethan." She dashed into her house, moving surprisingly fast.

"What are you doing here?" Kylie murmured, glancing after her neighbor as she hurried away. "It's still daylight, Mrs. Crowley is almost as big a gossip as Betty Randall, and—never mind, it's too late now."

"I'm back," Mrs. Crowley announced as she popped outside again.

Like they hadn't noticed.

She handed Ethan the calendar and a pen and he did his thing. "You're as nice as you are handsome," she gushed. "Thank you."

"My pleasure."

"Ethan, what do you—" Breaking off, Kylie

raised her eyebrows at Mrs. Crowley, but the nosy woman showed no sign of leaving.

"Don't let me stop you," she said, her gray eyes bright behind those glasses.

Enough already. "This is private business." Ethan grasped Kylie's arm. "Let's go inside."

As he guided her through the screen door she waved good bye to her neighbor. After crossing the threshold, she shut the front door behind them, turned the deadbolt, and pivoted toward him. "Do you have any idea what you've done? By tonight, everyone in town will know you were here. You could have at least warned me you were coming. What's so important that you couldn't pick up the phone?"

"I don't care if people know we're seeing each other. I missed you." He pulled her into a hot kiss. "Missed that."

She blinked dreamily. "Why didn't you say so?"

"I just did." He grinned. "By the way, I haven't seen that invoice yet."

Breaking away, she brushed the hair out of her eyes. "My plan was to send it by Friday, but I've been swamped. You wouldn't believe how many people were involved in collisions Thursday and Friday. Must've been the full moon. Then yesterday, I spent several hours with your sister. She's great, by the way. Not five minutes ago I emailed her bid. Believe it or not, I was about to calculate your bill. You'll have the invoice later today."

"I'll watch for it. I figured you and Heather would like each other. Did you meet Mike?"

"For a few minutes. He seems nice." She frowned. "What do you mean, you and I are seeing each other?"

Wasn't that obvious? "We are."

"As I recall, you said you'd be in touch when you came back from Portland, but we didn't get into the details. How was the concert? Did Mello draw a big crowd?"

"We did well enough that the club manager invited us to come back in October. Maybe I should've been more clear about you and me." Wanting to make his point, he tipped her chin up. "This strong pull between us—I want to explore it."

BETWEEN ETHAN'S riveting gaze and his fingers clasping her chin, Kylie wanted to climb his body and do some exploring of her own. Maybe Heather was right and he was ready for something more than single and free.

Wouldn't that be something. The most desirable man in town, wanting a real relationship with her... From somewhere inside her a longing for exactly that clamored to burst free. Unnerved, she pushed it away.

When she settled down it would be with a quiet, ordinary guy, not this gorgeous, sexy firefighter/saxophone-playing heartthrob. Anyway, she doubted Ethan had changed overnight. Still, it couldn't hurt to find out. "What you just said? You're short on details again and I'm not sure what you mean."

He angled her a look she couldn't read. "Don't overthink this, Kylie. As much as I want you, and I think about making love with you all the time, I won't lie. If you're looking for something deep and long-lasting, I'm not your guy."

The pang that bubbled up was likely indigestion from slathering an already buttery breakfast croissant with extra butter, not from disappointment. Regardless, she wanted him. "That's what I thought, and I'm fine with it."

He smiled into her eyes. "All right. We'll take things slow and when you're ready—"

"I'm ready now."

"But the last time we were together—"

"Since then, I've changed."

"That's a quick turnaround," he said. "Are you talking this minute now?"

"If you have protection with you. I don't."

His eyes went as dark as rich melted chocolate. "I always carry condoms."

"Excellent." Standing on her toes with her palms on his solid chest, she kissed the hollow of his neck, then licked it the way she'd wanted to that first time they'd met.

Groaning, he rocked against her. "Where's the bedroom?"

"This way." She reached for his hand.

14

"I didn't expect to find lace and flowers in here," Ethan said as he helped Kylie fold back the bedspread.

As desperate as she was to be with him, she paused. "No? What did you picture?"

"You, naked under me."

She trembled with anticipation. "If that's your idea of seduction, it's working."

"Babe, I'm just getting started." He tossed the spread onto a chair, then opened his arms. "Come here."

Nothing tender about this kiss. He devoured her mouth like a man starved for the taste of her. Despite the increasing intensity of their passion and delicious caresses, they remained fully clothed. Frustrated, she pushed him away.

"You changed your mind." Exhaling, he scrubbed his hand over his face. "That's okay, I can wait."

"You've got this all wrong. I don't want to wait.

You're moving too slow." She took off her shirt. Before it hit the floor, she'd removed her bra.

His shirt joined hers. His smoldering look made her nipples contract. "Who's seducing who?"

"Two can play—"

He stopped her with an erotic kiss that sizzled through every sensitive place in her body. Then they were both naked and in bed, engaged in a silent conversation. Touching, moaning, kissing, tasting everywhere.

Ethan was generous and thorough, satisfying her multiple times in multiple ways before he finally thrust into her, as deep as he could. Together, they shuddered to a powerful climax that obliterated all thoughts from Kylie's mind.

Afterward, lying motionless and sated, she roused herself and planted a kiss over his thudding heart. "I finally understand what 'the earth moved for me' means."

He let out a low, satisfied laugh and nuzzled the crook of her shoulder. "That was epic for me, too."

Treating her with genuine affection, he held her while they talked and laughed and dozed. They made love again. Limp as a noodle, Kylie lay with her head on his chest. His warm hand curled around her hip as if he wanted to keep her close. As if they were a real couple enjoying a lazy Sunday afternoon. Peaceful, relaxed, and content in ways she'd never dreamed of. Heaven.

Imagine having this to look forward to on a regular basis...

She cut off that train of thought. She and Ethan didn't have that kind of relationship. They never would.

All of a sudden, spending a whole afternoon in bed together seemed like a bad idea. Kylie sat up. "The afternoon is fading fast and I have things to do. Like tally up your bill."

"What time is it?" he asked, propping himself up on one arm.

"After 4:00."

He sat up beside her. "I didn't plan to stay this long. Guess we lost track of the time. " He tugged her a lock of her hair playfully. "Can't say that I mind."

She went soft inside. Why not continue to enjoy their phenomenal physical connection for as long as it lasted? She had no illusions about their relationship, so where was the harm?

On the way to the door after they dressed, Ethan's mouth quirked. "Do you think Mrs. Crowley will still be out there?"

"If she isn't, she'll be spying through her front window."

"In that case, I'll flash her a big smile." He kissed Kylie and left.

IT WAS a morning of drills and honing firefighting skills, some more challenging than others. Ethan's current task was a real bear. Lying on his stomach on a metal table and working by feel with a grinder wheel, he cut the rebar attached underneath. By the time he finished, sweat had beaded his face and his barely healed arms ached.

Adam gave him a thumbs-up. "You aced that. On to the next station."

No rest for the weary. The entire team had been at it for hours, each man moving from one drill to another.

By the time Adam announced the end of the session, Ethan was more than ready for lunch. As he tromped upstairs to the kitchen he received a text from Kylie.

Guess who ordered business cards today?

"I'll be up shortly," he told the crew. Smiling, he hung back and called her. "Congrats on landing the job with my sister," he said when she answered.

"News travels fast. Did she tell you?"

"No. I saw your text and put two and two together."

"You're one smart guy. I'm super excited."

"I like when you're excited. It's hot." He lowered his voice. "Sunday was fantastic. I keep thinking about us together in your bed."

She moaned softly. "Don't, Ethan. I'm sitting

outside on a bench near my office, eating my sandwich and trying to look composed."

"I won't keep you long. It's lunchtime here too, and I'm running on empty."

"Busy morning?"

"Drills and more drills." He told her about a few.

"No wonder you're hungry. Before I forget, you should know that I renewed my prescription for birth control pills."

"I approve. Hey, Max and Hank, two of my crewmates, are coming over Thursday to take a look at my new, improved office. You never know, one of them may decide to hire you."

"You're good at drumming up business for me."

"That's easy—I like your work." Liked her, period. Which was okay, as long as he didn't make a damn fool of himself. Not gonna happen. He wanted her something fierce, that's what this was about. "Can I come over Thursday night?"

"Please do. I'm picking up my business cards after work, but I should be home by seven."

"I can't wait to see them. Hell, I can't wait to see you. Don't plan on getting much sleep that night."

"Mm," she purred. "I—oh, shoot! I just spilled my soda all over myself. Gotta go."

Ethan disconnected and headed upstairs, already counting the hours until they were together.

After stopping for a quick bite to eat and picking up her brand-new business cards, Kylie arrived home later than she'd expected. Ethan was already there, chatting in the yard with Mrs. Crowley, who hung on his every word. Clearly, he'd made her elderly neighbor's evening.

She wasn't the only one smitten. The more time Kylie spent with the big, irresistible man, the more she liked him. As long as she didn't lose her heart...

She wouldn't. Theirs was a relationship based on sex, with no illusions and no expectations beyond the here and now. Knowing exactly where she stood lowered the chances of future hurt and disappointment. She'd be a complete idiot to fall for him.

The warmth in his eyes made her knees wobble. "Sorry I'm late," she said, a little breathless. "The printer couldn't locate my order, and finding it took a little while. Are you ready for this? Ta-da." She opened the box of business cards and handed cards to both Ethan and Mrs. Crowley."

Ethan whistled. "Classy."

"What's Clutter Buster?" Mrs. Crowley asked, frowning at the card.

"The business I've started on the side. I help people organize their things."

"I had no idea. What kinds of things?"

"Closets, kitchens, basements—you name it."

"I could use help with my pantry."

"You can't go wrong with Kylie," Ethan said. "She's the best. I should know—I was her first client. She did an awesome job on my home office."

He showered her with a ten-thousand-watt grin that lit her up inside. He was proud of her and not afraid to show it. Such a turn-on. Suddenly, she ached to be alone with him. "It's chilly out here and I'm ready to go inside," she said. "Good night, Mrs. Crowley. I'll talk to you later about your pantry."

"Anytime. Good night, you two."

"Thanks for that plug," she said on the way inside.

"I meant every word. Max and Hank were impressed with the changes you made in my office. I'll bet they both decide they need your services. They should meet you. I want you to meet the whole crew. Hey, I just thought of a great way to make that happen—I'll host a cookout Saturday, a last hurrah to summer."

Kylie wanted to, but... "That sounds fun, only I'm scheduled to be at Heather and Mike's Saturday. I'm not sure how late I'll be there."

"Not past six. Come over when you're done."

"Okay."

"Excellent." Ethan locked the door behind them, set her things down, and kissed her until she was lost in a haze of desire. "Damn, I've missed that."

"It's only been a few days," she teased.

"Feels like a hell of a lot longer."

He seemed lighter and more carefree than usual. She squinted at him. "Something is different about you."

"You can see that? Last night, magic happened. You know that Rafe and Jillian are getting married in two weeks and I've been stuck on that song for them. When I sat down to work on it after dinner, the words poured out. Then this afternoon after Hank and Max left, I started composing the music. It's coming along well. I'm beginning to think I'll get it done and recorded in time."

"That's great news. Sometimes you need a deadline to jumpstart things."

"It's not the deadline. It's you—you're my muse."

Caught off guard, Kylie blinked. She'd never in a million years imagined Ethan would— Wait.

Was he saying he cared more than she thought? Unbelievable how badly she wanted that. Her heart pounding, she raised her eyebrows.

He appeared to be almost as startled by his pronouncement as she was. "What I mean is, thanks to the great sex we've been having, my creative block is gone."

Nope, his feelings for her hadn't changed. Deep down, she'd known. Masking her disappointment, she slid her finger slowly down his chest and wet her lips. "Happy to help. I'm available anytime."

His eyes went dark and intent. "How about now?"

She reached for him.

~

AFTER SPENDING an enjoyable day organizing Heather and Mike's closet and bedroom on Saturday, Kylie went home to shower and change before heading to Ethan's. She considered packing an overnight bag, but hesitated. Despite spending a delicious night together on Thursday, he hadn't invited her to stay at his place tonight. Maybe he needed a break.

Not wanting to seem clingy or put him on the spot, she left the suitcase at home and brought only her purse and the package of cornbread she'd picked up early this morning. On the drive to Ethan's she congratulated herself for playing smart. By outward appearances she looked that way. Under the surface, not so much.

From the moment Ethan had sung her praises to Mrs. Crowley Thursday night she'd been in trouble. In the wee hours Friday morning, after making slow, tender love with him, the remains of her no-illusions, no-expectations, enjoy the physical for as long as it lasts philosophy had crumbled like summer dust, her emotions too overwhelming to fight.

She loved him.

Calling herself reckless and stupid for putting herself in emotional danger—there was no question she'd end up alone and in a world of hurt—didn't change a thing.

Ethan had no idea, and if she could help it he never would.

His front door was unlocked, but there was no one in the house. She heard voices and followed the sounds to the back yard. Ethan stood near a smoking grill, flanked by four handsome firefighters and nearly as many women.

When he caught sight of her his eyes lit up, setting off all kinds of crazy inside.

"I finally made it," she said, sounding normal instead of wild with love and longing. She held out the cornbread. "Where should I put this?"

Ethan set it on a small table on the patio. "You can put it with the other side dishes in the house after you meet everyone. Not all the crew could make it tonight, but this is a start. Hey guys, meet

Kylie." He put his arm around her and made the introductions.

From the start, she felt comfortable and accepted. They were full of praise for the improvements she'd made to Ethan's office. Hank's girlfriend, Deanna, asked Kylie to help organize the shed she used as storage for her bed and breakfast. Megan, involved with Max, wanted some of her business cards to share with some of her teacher friends. Tony's partner Summer, who was pregnant and radiant, promised to spread the word.

"You'll meet the rest of the crew at Rafe and Jillian's party in a couple of weeks," Rob said. "You're coming, right?"

Did Ethan even want her there? He hadn't mentioned it. Keeping her expression neutral and any assumptions at bay, Kylie glanced at him. "I've never met them, so I don't know. Am I invited?"

He drew her closer to his side. "You sure are. You're my plus one."

"Then, yes, I'll be there."

Fall air nipped the evening, and they all ate at the dining room table.

"I need a hand in the kitchen," Ethan told her at the end of the meal.

"I'm happy to help too," Deanna offered.

Ethan shook his head. "Sip your beer and relax."

"What do you need?" Kylie asked as she followed him into the kitchen.

"For starters, this." He backed her to the wall, plastered his body to hers, and gave her a smoldering kiss.

When they came up for air, she'd wrapped one leg around his hips with no recollection of doing it. Regretfully, she untangled herself. "Did you have to do that? I'm about to go up in flames."

"That's one of the things I like about you, Kylie. You catch fire as fast as I do." He nibbled the sensitive curve between her neck and shoulder, setting off all kinds of hunger inside, then backed away with the cocky grin that always caused cartwheels in her stomach. "How did it go at my sister's?"

"She and Mike seemed satisfied. They wanted cards to hand out to their friends."

"Everyone wants you, " he growled, pulling her into a fierce hug. "But you're mine."

Words to warm her heart, only she knew better. His feelings were temporary, hers weren't. Hiding her love wasn't easy.

Why was she putting herself through this? She'd plead exhaustion and leave soon.

"Everything okay?" Ethan asked.

"It's been a long day. I'm tired."

"You'll forget all about that when we're alone. Let's get the dessert on the table and move this party along. I'll grab the plates. You bring the cookies and cupcakes."

16

"As much as I enjoy hanging with my crewmates, I'm glad they're finally gone," Ethan told Kylie when the last of his guests departed. He wanted her now and all night long. "Why don't you grab your overnight bag from the car."

"I didn't bring one."

He didn't hide what he thought of that. And cursed himself for calling her his muse the other night. The look on her face... He'd never meant to tell her, his own words catching him by surprise. He'd sounded like a total dweeb. Blame it on his inner dork for momentarily breaking free. He couldn't remember the last time that had happened. For damn sure it wouldn't again.

"I assumed you were going to stay," he said. "I've shared your bed several times but you've never tried mine. It's a great bed, and I guarantee you'll find it to your liking."

"We spent Thursday night together, and twice

in one week seems like a lot." Frowning, she brushed at something on her sleeve. "Also, I have tons to do at home—laundry and cleaning, and I need groceries for the week. If I want to get that all done before Monday I need to get up early in the morning."

Ethan didn't buy the excuses, unless she wasn't as into him as he was her. He was nowhere near ready to give up what they shared, not by a long shot. Besides, he'd quickly shifted the credit for his music breakthrough to their great sex, after which they'd enjoyed a whole night of it. Between that and her red-hot response to him earlier this evening, she seemed every bit as on-board with their relationship as he was.

She had a valid point, though. He rarely spent a full night with anyone.

But Kylie wasn't just anyone.

"Up to you," he said. "But I want you here and I think I can convince you to stay."

"Oh? How?"

"I know what you like."

As he'd anticipated, she made a breathless sound. "I don't have to spend the night to try out your bed."

Time to get serious. "I crave you like an addict craves drugs. I want you all night." He traced her nipple with his finger, letting out a low laugh when she moaned. "You're just as hot for me. I have band rehearsal next Wednesday, Thursday, and Friday night. Our sessions tend to run late.

Tonight will be our last time together for a while."

Frown lines creased her forehead. "I don't remember you rehearsing every night before Portland."

"I skipped that Wednesday because you came over to work on the office, but we rehearsed Thursday and Friday." He added an incentive sure to tempt her. "I happen to have a brand-new can of chocolate Reddi-wip in the pantry."

"You're planning to make sundaes?"

"Off your body."

Heat shimmered in her eyes. She touched her tongue to her upper lip, reminding him of when she used her tongue on him. Instant hard-on. "Can I do that to you, too?"

God, he wanted her. "Count on it. No whipped cream unless you stay."

"You're a very persuasive man. All right, I'll stay, but I'll be up early to get home."

"That's okay with me."

Unwilling to let go of her, he pulled her with him to the pantry and grabbed the can. He wanted to take her to his bed but she unbuttoned her top and stepped out of her jeans, and they never made it out of the pantry.

Sometime later, sticky with the remains of Reddi-wip clinging to their skin, he carried her toward the bathroom. "We're a mess. Care to join me in a shower?"

"Why yes, Mr. Goldberg."

"That was another good idea," she said as he wrapped her in a towel after the hottest shower of his life.

He flashed a big smile. "I have a lot more in mind and we have the whole night ahead."

While he recovered they lay in bed, talking easily. The next time they made love he took his time. They fell asleep, spoon style. Before dawn he woke up hard and desperate to be inside her. "Are you awake?" he whispered, cupping her breasts from behind.

"I am now. You're aroused." She turned to face him.

Best morning sex ever.

"Mello is playing at Lucky Joe's Saturday night," he told her sometime later.

"That's why you scheduled all those rehearsals. I wondered, but I was a little distracted and forgot to ask."

"Distracting you is fun." In the dim predawn light he kissed the top of her head.

She smiled. "I like your fun. I'm amazed the band rehearses so much."

"Practice makes perfect and we always give our best, especially at Lucky Joe's. We played our very first gig there. We'll do a few other things too. I need the band's help smoothing out the rough patches in Rafe and Jillian's song. Hey, why don't you come to the concert? It's gonna be a great show."

Instead of jumping at the chance, she shook

her head. "I don't think so, Ethan. There's sure to be a reporter there covering the concert. Everyone will be taking photos and I don't want to call attention to myself or us again."

The thought of her standing among his fans and watching him perform was irresistible. "Understandable, but if you stay in the back of the room and we pretend we don't know each other, people will leave you alone."

"It's possible, but I need to think about it. Can I let you know?"

"No problem." Not true. For some reason he needed her there the way he needed to play his sax. "I really want you to come," he added. *Way to put yourself out there, dorkface.*

"Oh? Why is that?"

Because she mattered, but he wasn't about to lay his neck on the line even further. "Do I need a reason? It'll be fun."

She averted her gaze and glanced down as if she didn't want to look at him. Confused, he frowned. "Something on your mind?"

"No."

Her head remained bowed. He tucked her hair behind her ears, then lifted her chin. "You can tell me anything."

"I'm good." She shifted out of his grasp.

Whatever it was, she wasn't going to talk about it and he couldn't make her. He sat up. "I need coffee. Stay put—I'll bring you a cup when it's ready."

"I'm tempted, but those chores won't keep forever." Reaching for the towel she'd dropped by the side of the bed after last night's shower, she wrapped it around her and sat up beside him. "I should go home and get started." She padded out of the bedroom to collect her clothes from the kitchen where she'd left them hours ago.

What the hell? Knowing he'd blown the end of a great night yet clueless how, Ethan stepped into a pair of jeans. He toed into his sneakers, then determined to end their time together on a better note, headed toward the kitchen to walk her out.

IN THE GRAY light of the advancing dawn the earliest birds were beginning to sing. As Ethan escorted Kylie to her car, despite her insistence that she was perfectly capable of going by herself, she sensed a fine tension in him that hadn't been there earlier. Since she'd first arrived at the barbecue, he'd been sweet and affectionate. Making love with her in so many ways—with and without whipped cream, on top and under her, fast and desperate, slow and tender.

Although her feelings for him had grown to the point that she had trouble containing them, she'd managed. Then he'd invited her to his concert, so serious and intent about it. She'd been certain he wanted something deeper than a brief romance, had gone giddy with hope, even more so than when he'd called her his muse. But like the other night the moment had passed, flattening those hopes and leaving her with a heavy heart.

Loving him made her ache for a future that would never be. Maybe her face wasn't recognizable, but why risk putting herself in the spotlight again for a man who didn't love her?

"Kylie—" he started.

"Ethan—" she said at the same time.

He gestured to her. "You first."

"I'm going to pass on the concert."

"Figured as much. You're upset and I don't know why."

His eyes pleaded with her and she considered telling him the truth. But she couldn't humiliate herself like that. "You didn't do anything."

She meant it. He'd always been straightforward about their relationship. The sadness she felt was her own doing.

"All right." He scrubbed his hand over his face. "The invitation stands. If you change your mind, let me know."

17

"You missed out on a good time at Ethan's Saturday night," Rob told the crew over Monday breakfast at the station. "Kylie's cool."

Ethan couldn't argue with that.

"Wish I'd been there and met her," Liam said.

Ethan shrugged. "You'll get your chance at Rafe and Jillian's party." Provided she still wanted to come.

"Ah, she's your plus one." Liam squinted at him. "You seem bummed."

"I am. I invited her to my concert next Saturday. First she said she needed to think about it, then she turned me down."

"As gun-shy as she is about publicity, can you blame her?"

"We had that figured out. People know her name but even with the photo they don't know what she looks like. She was going to stand in the back and we'd act like we didn't know each other. She knew I wanted her there."

His crewmates traded knowing looks. Liam ran his hand over his shaved head. "What'd you do to her, man?"

"Wish I knew. I treated her nice—real nice. I didn't hear any complaints." Laughter, yes, and plenty of moaning and pleading for him to hurry and satisfy her. Ethan doubted he'd ever get enough of that, of her. "The next morning she did a complete turnaround. She wouldn't say why."

"You're really messed up about that."

Ethan slumped in his seat. "Yeah."

"Look at you. You're totally gone over her."

No kidding.

Damn. Was he in love with Kylie?

He was, for the first time in his life. Blindsided, he sat back hard.

"She doesn't know how you feel, am I right?" Liam asked.

Ethan shook his head.

"She needs to know."

"You're one to talk. You've been carrying a torch for a woman who dropped your ass over a year ago."

Liam gave him the finger. "I'm trying to help."

"Yeah, I know." Having barely digested the staggering fact that he loved Kylie, Ethan needed time to think about the next step. If she rejected him... At the thought he went cold all over. Not gonna go there, not here, not now. He checked his watch. "Our meeting starts in five. We'd best clean up and get downstairs to the apparatus bay."

By Tuesday evening, after heavy soul-searching, Ethan faced up to the facts. First, despite his best efforts, his inner dork was here to stay. Second, no matter what he did or how many women wanted him today, the old scars of rejection never quite faded away.

Screw them both. Kylie owned his heart and he wanted a serious relationship with her. Now he needed to figure out how to tell her without making her run off. Ready for advice, and not from Liam or any of his single crewmates, he sought out Tony. Recently, the one-time player had committed fully to his girl.

After dinner, Ethan pulled him aside. "With you and Summer... How did that go down?"

"Well, she *was* pregnant." His buddy laughed. "Still, I was pretty thick-headed. I almost blew my chances with her."

"But you didn't."

"Because I wised up. I told her I loved her and that I wanted a lifetime together. Smartest thing I ever did."

"You weren't worried she'd reject you?"

"You'd better believe I was. From the get-go she claimed she wasn't interested in that kind of relationship. So yeah, I was nervous as hell. But there was too much at stake to let that stop me.

Now we're solid. Be clear and speak straight from the heart—you'll do fine."

Reassured, Ethan nodded. "I will. Thanks, man."

By Wednesday morning, the whole crew knew about his plans.

"When are you going to tell her?" Liam asked.

"I have rehearsals all week, so it'll be after the concert. But I'll let her know we need to talk."

KYLIE HAD MADE plans to meet Cheryl for dinner Wednesday, a sisters' night out at last. And a good thing, since a few hours ago Ethan had texted that Sunday, the day following the concert, they needed to get together and talk. Code for breaking up.

As yet, Kylie hadn't replied. She was too heartsick, plus she wanted her sister's take on the situation. They met at Barclay's, a restaurant low-key enough for uninterrupted conversation.

"No husband, no son—this is the life," Cheryl marveled over cocktails. "It's a shame we both have to work tomorrow. Otherwise, we could stay out late. At least we're out together. Feels like forever since we've talked. I'm dying to hear about Ethan and Clutter Buster."

Not wanting to begin the evening talking about Ethan, which was guaranteed to be a downer, Kylie motioned for her sister to start.

"We'll talk about me later. I want to hear about you."

"I have lots of news. This is exciting—I finally got an order for soap the other day from that company in Portland I've been courting the past two years. If the soaps sell well and they reorder, my business could double. But then, that's why I opened a factory and hired a good team." Bubbling and animated, Cheryl launched into the details.

Kylie was thrilled for her. "That's terrific."

"I know! Lucas said the funniest thing the other day. He came home from preschool talking a mile a minute about a visit from two firefighters. Tony and Gus—do you know them?"

"I met Tony the other night."

"Lucky you. I'll bet the teachers enjoyed having those gorgeous men at their school. Anyway, the kids got to climb aboard the fire engine. Lucas came home saying he loved that truck so much, his eyes hurt." Cheryl laughed. "Who knows where he came up with that one."

Kylie smiled and shook her head. "He's so adorable."

The salads arrived and Cheryl continued. "You'll find this interesting. Saturday night, Patrick and I are going out for dinner and a movie. You'll never guess who's babysitting."

"The high school girl down the street?"

"No—Dad and Virginia."

Kylie didn't hide her amazement. "Both of them? Together?"

"I'm as surprised as you. They're not splitting up, after all."

"I never in a million years... Miracles do happen."

"Amen, and wouldn't it be wonderful if Dad finally got his happily ever after with Virginia? I've always liked her."

"Same here." Kylie held up her drink. "To miracles."

Cheryl joined her in a celebratory salute, then set her glass down. "I've caught you up on my life. Now it's your turn."

"Clutter Buster is off to a good start. So far I've had two actual clients and interest from several other people, all through word of mouth." Thanks to Ethan. "Here, take a few business cards."

"Very professional. I'll hand them out."

"You're the best."

"I want you to be successful with this. Tell me about Ethan."

It was time. Leaning forward, Kylie lowered her voice. "Things aren't going well."

With a stricken expression, Cheryl set down her fork. "Don't tell me you're not seeing each other anymore. I thought sure you two—I'm sorry."

"We haven't broken up. Yet."

Yet?" Cheryl echoed, all eyes.

Kylie's troubles poured out. "The worst has happened— I'm in love with him. I tried so hard to keep my emotions in check."

"I doubt anyone can fight their own heart and win. Awesome that you're in love! It's been a long time. I'm a little lost, though. What makes you think you and Ethan might break up?"

"He's always been honest with me, reminding me more than once that he's not interested in committing to one woman. He likes being single. For a while I was okay with that. I enjoyed our no-strings relationship for what it was. I had no expectations and I didn't have to worry about whether I could trust him or stress over what tomorrow might bring. But I've changed. I've tried to hide my feelings, but you know how bad I am at that. I'm nervous he'll figure it out." Kylie bit her lip. "He may already have."

"You're worried he'll break up with you if he knows?"

Kylie nodded. "Earlier this afternoon, I had a text from him. He wants to talk, and you know what that means." With her finger she made a slicing motion across her throat.

"Not always. Has he been pulling away from you?"

She thought about the other night, the way he'd loved her and held her afterward, and shook her head.

"To me, it sounds as if he has feelings for you."

"Yes—he likes me."

Cheryl nodded. "There you go."

"For now. Ethan has his pick of women. At the moment he's chosen me, but sooner or later he'll want someone new and move on. That's the way it is." Unable to finish her salad, she pushed the plate aside.

"Have you ever stopped to think that he's falling in love too?"

"If he cared that much, wouldn't he at least hint at it? He hasn't said one word about a future together."

"So he hasn't used the L word. That doesn't mean he isn't feeling it."

"Come on, Cheryl, he's never been in a long-term relationship."

Maybe you're his one and only. Some guys are wired that way."

Kylie snorted. "I'm not that naïve."

"If he's the kind of man who doesn't realize his true feelings, he may need a nudge from you. Start by admitting yours, then he'll do the same."

At the mere thought, Kylie felt her heart stutter in horror. "Um, no. We made a deal not to get serious, and I don't think he'd be happy to find out I'm in love with him."

"When are you planning to have this talk?"

"This is a crazy busy week for him—he's rehearsing a lot for a concert at Lucky Joe's Saturday night. We're meeting Sunday."

"That gives you time to do some thinking."

Kylie sighed. "Last time I saw him he invited me to Lucky Joe's to see him play."

"He wouldn't have done that if he wanted to break up."

"I don't know if he still wants me there. Besides, you know how I feel about calling attention to myself. I told him I wasn't going."

Her sister gaped at her. "Then change your mind."

"So I go and people figure out we're a couple. Then we break up and Ethan finds a new girlfriend. Does that sound fun to you?"

"What makes you think anyone cares who Ethan is involved with? His fans are more interested in his music. And don't you think this break-up thing is a little premature? Seems to me you're putting the cart before the horse."

"True, but I can't help it. What am I supposed to do now?"

"Take a deep breath and back away from your dark place. I get that you have abandonment issues. Heck, first Mom left us, then Gordon. And they both did it in very public ways."

"Ya think? But I don't see myself as abandoned. Hurt, yes."

"You were definitely abandoned. Speaking for myself, I'd rather take a chance with the man I love than suffer through the pain than end up lonely and alone. I don't think you want that either."

Kylie sighed. "Paint a dreary picture, why don't you?"

"I'm trying to make a point. If miracles exist for Dad and he gets his happy ending, why can't you? Bad things happened to you, but don't let them hold you back. You deserve to love and be loved."

"I agree, but it's not that easy."

"Nothing worth fighting for is. Don't forget, Mom left me too, and I've also had my share of broken hearts. Instead of letting those setbacks stop me, I tried again with Patrick. Remember when we first got together? I wasn't sure about him but I took a chance with him anyway. Like any couple we've had our ups and downs, but I've never regretted my decision. If you love Ethan, you owe it to yourself to be honest with him."

A t home after leaving the restaurant, Kylie replied to Ethan's text. She agreed to meet him Sunday for coffee at the café of his choice. The location didn't matter, as long as they met in a public place, where she was less likely to cry.

Over the next few days, she mulled over her sister's advice—and dismissed it. As unappealing as the thought was of spending her life without Ethan, she couldn't tell him she loved him. Too risky. Anyway, if he wanted to end the relationship, what was the point in thinking about it?

Friday night she stuffed herself with caramel popcorn drizzled with chocolate and bingeing on the previous year's worth of *Project Runway* episodes, a nice escape from her own drama. Being alone had its perks.

At some point in the dead of night, during an ad in the second to last episode, she closed her eyes for minute and fell asleep. She woke with a start. Disoriented and thinking she was in bed with Ethan, she reached for him and almost tumbled off the sofa. All by herself.

Hating the empty feeling inside and realizing she had an awful crick in her neck—shouldn't have drifted off with her head on the armrest—she struggled up and checked her watch. Already past noon, way later than she normally slept.

After taking an aspirin for her neck, she stood under the spray of a hot shower to loosen her muscles. Too bad Ethan wasn't with her, massaging away the kinks and making her laugh. Giving her pleasure.

She missed him so much, her heart ached. So much, she considered calling and inviting him to come over after the concert. But he might break up with her. No sense causing that kind of pain just yet.

Better think about that over coffee and breakfast—make that lunch.

She barely tasted her cheese toast for thinking about Ethan. Honest, sincere, and kind, he was exactly the man she'd always dreamed of making a life with—aside from his fame—but no one was perfect. Cheryl was right. If Kylie let her abandonment issues get in the way she'd never find love. She owed it to herself to follow her heart, let her love for him out, and give him the chance to love her back.

Funny how the thought no longer scared her. Well, a little, but he was worth fighting for.

And if the relationship didn't last? At least she'd know she'd been brave enough to try.

Once she made up her mind, she was eager to talk to Ethan. Now, if possible. His phone went straight to voicemail. He was probably busy getting ready for tonight. What she wanted to say was too important to leave in a voice message, let alone a text. "Call me," she said and disconnected.

The rest of the day she cleaned house, ran errands, and dreamed of a future with Ethan. By dinnertime she still hadn't heard from him. Refusing to let that stop her she called again, and left another message. "I think we should talk tonight instead of tomorrow, if possible before the concert. I'm leaving shortly. Watch for me."

She threw on fresh clothes, headed out the door, and drove to Lucky Joe's.

AN HOUR before Mello was due on stage, Ethan joined Rob and Liam for dinner at Lucky Joe's. The other four members of the band planned to arrive closer to showtime.

"Did Kylie change her mind about tonight?" Liam asked over the meal.

Not that Ethan had heard. He glanced at his phone and remembered he'd set it to Do Not Disturb during sound check earlier. As soon as he restored the setting to normal, messages popped up. At the moment, only two interested him, both from Kylie. He listened. "She'll be here."

Liam grinned. "I finally get to meet her."

"She didn't say if she'd come to the concert, only that she wants to talk to me now instead of tomorrow." Which sounded an awful lot like she wanted to break up, and that hit like a punch to the chest.

No longer smiling, Liam shook his head. "Man, you need a plan B."

"I'll stick to the one I have." Ethan intended to give his all to convince her to stay with him, speaking straight from the heart, like Tony said. "I'm heading outside to wait for her."

He exited through the employees-only door at the rear of the building and stepped into the twilit, rapidly cooling evening. Years ago the club had annexed a vacant lot in the back for spillover parking. Already it was more than half full, a sure sign of a packed show tonight. He searched for Kylie's car but didn't see it. She wasn't out front either.

Sliding his cell phone from his pocket, he called her. Her phone rang and rang. He was about to leave a message when she answered.

"Ethan? There's no place to park in front. I'm just pulling into a slot near the fence behind the building."

Shoring himself up for what was to come, he pivoted back toward the annexed lot. "I'll meet you at the employees-only door."

He rounded the corner and saw her hurrying toward him, the building's outdoor lighting illuminating her ruffled hair in the gentle evening breeze. Drinking in the sight of her, he met her halfway.

"Ethan, we—" She held up her finger, signaling him to wait, and paused to catch her breath, as winded as if she'd run to reach him.

He took advantage of the moment. "First, hear me out."

Her eyes widened. "Wait—please. You can't break up with me, Ethan."

Certain he'd misheard her, he gave her a sideways look. "Come again?"

She inhaled, then exhaled, then murmured "Here goes" under her breath. "When we agreed not to get serious, I didn't know my feelings for you would grow as much as they did. Then I tried to convince myself I wasn't falling for you. I know I convinced you. But it was only a matter of time before you figured out the truth and left me.

"Then Cheryl pointed out that I have abandonment issues, and I realized I do. I don't want to be controlled by them. I love you, Ethan. There, I said it." She drew herself up straight and held her head high as if ready to ward off a blow. "If you still want to break up with me, get it over with fast."

Her courage amazed him. That and her words. She loved him. He laughed softly. "You're always surprising me, Kylie, in a good way. I don't want to break up with you." Ready to bare his heart, he cupped her face between his hands.

"OMG, there's Ethan with Kylie Treadwell, the woman from the photograph!" a female fan shrieked.

Ethan had been so intent on what Kylie was saying he'd forgotten where they were. He glanced around. A group of fans had gathered, their phones out and pointed at him and Kylie. At the same time a familiar click nearby drew his attention. Hell, was that the reporter covering the concert while Betsy Pappas was on leave? As he let go of Kylie the camera's flash exploded.

19

Where had the reporter and all those people come from? Startled, Kylie ducked her head but it was too late. Her face felt hot and she knew she was blushing.

"Don't let them get to you." With tenderness Ethan smoothed the hair out of her eyes, instantly calming her. "The lady and I need some privacy," he said in a voice loud enough to carry. He made a show of lacing his fingers with hers.

"Don't let us bother you," someone called out.

The crowd, which had grown larger, laughed and stayed put, lighting the night as they snapped photos with their phones. Nearby, the reporter captured everything.

Kylie hated it. On the other hand, Ethan didn't want to break up. Fortified by that and his big, warm fingers between hers, she held on tight.

To her relief, the club manager and a bouncer showed up and began to herd the group toward the club entrance. Someone must have alerted them. Rob and Liam, a firefighter she hadn't met but recognized from the calendar, also showed up, along with Ethan's band mates.

Ethan introduced Kylie, then nodded at the last of the crowd. "You should join them,"

Liam elbowed Rob and they followed the fans.

"We're due on stage soon," one of Ethan's band mates commented as they too turned to leave. "We'll start the set to keep the fans from getting too restless but they'll want you."

Ethan nodded. "I'll be there in five."

Except for the reporter they were finally alone. With a warning look at the man, he tugged her behind a large fat bush near the employees' door. "Alone at last. I think. Hold on while I make sure the reporter isn't hiding someplace."

Moments later he returned. "He's gone. I believe it's my turn to talk." He clasped both her hands in his. "You're my everything, the most important person in my life. There are times when you irritate the hell out of me, but you keep me on my toes and I wouldn't have it any other way. What I mean is, I love you too."

"Really?"

"Really. Come here, you." Ethan kissed her deeply, then broke away and rested his forehead on hers. "Got that?"

Dreamy-eyed, Kylie nodded. "You have no idea how amazing I feel. I knew you liked me but you never said much about it. That night I stayed at your house you pulled back and things got tense... It made me nervous. Then when you texted that you wanted to talk, I assumed you wanted to end things."

"You're right about me pulling back. Instead of telling you how much you matter, I hid my feelings—baggage from my dork days. I'm still a dork at heart and I'm cool with that. In other words from now on, you'll be getting an earful, some of it awful corny."

"I can't wait." Filled with love and joy, she touched his face. "What a pair we make. Me with my abandonment issues and you with your dork baggage."

"Just a couple of lovebirds winging our way toward the future. Told you I'm corny."

"I like it. Since we're being honest... I've been in love with you since you stopped by to see my business cards and talked me up to Mrs. Crowley."

"She's all right. And she likes me."

"Wait until she finds out about us."

Ethan snorted. "As often as I'm at your place? I suspect she already knows."

As Kylie lost herself in another kiss, the club manager opened the rear door and the crowd's chant spilled out. "Ethan! Ethan! Ethan!"

"No telling what they'll do if you don't get in here," the manager said.

"On my way." Ethan caught hold of Kylie's hand. "By now the fans know who you are, but if it makes you more comfortable, stay in the back of the room. Just please, come in."

That people recognized her made being there all the harder. "I'll come because you want me there. But I'm going to stay in the shadows."

~

WHEN THE CONCERT ended Ethan bounded off the stage toward Kylie. "You're still standing and you don't seem at all nervous."

"I'm not." And wasn't that a wonder. After staying in the back of the room for all of a few minutes, the crowd had begun chanting her name just as they had Ethan's. When she started forward, they parted to let her through and called out greetings.

Exhilarating, even if she did prefer to avoid publicity. Every female in the audience gave her envious looks. Kylie enjoyed that, too, and could hardly believe the multi-talented, handsome male had chosen her over them all.

"That was the best concert I've ever been to," she told him. "And not because I love you. Well, that's part of it."

He grinned. "You'd better. Listen, I need to finish up with my band mates backstage and make a call. I may be awhile. If you don't want to wait..."

"I don't mind. I'll sip another glass of wine."

By the time he returned, her glass was empty

and she was fighting the urge to check for photos online. "Sorry about that."

"No problem. Who did you call? Heather? Your parents?"

He shook his head. "I'll talk to them tomorrow. I'm not saying who I phoned. It's a surprise."

Something in his face made her want to giggle. "For me? Give me a hint?"

"Uh-uh. You'll have to wait and see. We have a lot to talk about tonight. Your place or mine?"

"Your bed is bigger."

"But your house is closer. I have to be alone with you ASAP."

"My house it is."

20

When Kylie woke up Sunday, Ethan's side of the bed was empty. They'd spent a wonderful night making plans and loving each other. She heard noises in the kitchen and smelled coffee. Still naked, she shrugged into her robe, tied the sash, and padded barefoot to find him.

Sexy in jeans and nothing else, he greeted her with a melting smile, followed by a tender kiss. "Morning, sleepy head. I made coffee."

He fixed her a mug exactly as she liked it—a splash of milk and no sugar. She could get used to this. She sat down. The paper was open to the Arts & Life section, no doubt showing her and Ethan in the very private moment after he'd said he wasn't going to break up with her. Her good mood fading, Kylie averted her eyes and pushed the paper away.

"Don't you want to look at the photo and read the story?"

"I'd rather not."

"You need to."

"See our private moment made public? And God knows what that reporter wrote about us. Please don't make me."

"Would I steer you wrong? I thought you trusted me."

A bad habit she meant to put behind her. "I do, completely. I'll look at it after I fortify myself with coffee."

Her cell rang. Filled with dread, she checked the screen and groaned. "It's Cheryl. She's seen the picture. I don't want to talk to her now, but if I ignore her she'll call back until I answer." Mentally squaring her shoulders, she picked up. "Hi, Cheryl."

Her sister laughed. "Didn't I tell you? I'm so happy for you!"

"What are you talking about?"

"You haven't read the paper?"

"Not yet. Ugh."

"Do it *now*."

"With you and Ethan on my case, I don't have much choice." He slid the paper in front of her and she gave in.

The photo of her gazing into Ethan's eyes as he cupped her face in his big hands wasn't so bad. Neither was the headline. "Love in the air at Lucky Joe's last night," she read aloud, then frowned at Ethan. "How did the reporter come up with that?"

"He's the guy I phoned after the concert. I know you hate publicity and I wanted to make it better."

"I heard that," Cheryl said. "Put me on speaker, Kylie."

Kylie sighed. "All right, it's on. "

"Hi, Ethan. I'm Cheryl. You're a keeper. If Kylie doesn't hold onto you, I promise to nag her forever."

"You don't have to," Kylie said, and blew Ethan a kiss. "I love this man with all my heart. And Ethan, you're right—I don't mind this kind of publicity so much."

"That's good. From time to time, you'll no doubt be photographed with me."

"Will we be kissing?"

"I intend to kiss you every chance I get."

He was about to make good on that when Cheryl interrupted. "When do I get to meet you, Ethan?"

His mouth hovered over Kylie's and she barely suppressed a moan. "We're kind of busy right now," he told Cheryl. "Let's talk later."

He disconnected and set the phone to Do Not Disturb. Desperate for him, Kylie slipped out of her robe.

His eyes almost bugged out of his head. "I figured you put on PJs."

"Why bother when I knew I'd be taking them right off? You said something about kissing me?"

They started toward the bedroom and ended up having wild sex against the wall.

"God, I love being inside you. I love you, period," Ethan murmured against her neck.

Kylie didn't think she'd ever get tired of hearing those words. "I love you too."

"Do you have time to stop by the station after work tomorrow? You can say hi to the guys who know you and meet Captain Comings and the rest of the crew. Unless a call comes in, we'll all be there."

"I thought I was going to meet everyone at Rafe and Jillian's party next weekend."

"Yeah, but this is a good excuse for you to stop by."

"The captain won't mind?"

"Are you kidding? He's been hearing about you for weeks."

"I'll be over right after work." Kylie kissed him. "How did I get so lucky?"

"We both did, and we're in for the ride of a lifetime."

She smiled. "I trust you on that."

THE END

THANK you for letting me share my stories with you!

. . .

IF YOU ENJOYED **MR. SEPTEMBER,** help others find this book by recommending it to your friends and by writing a review. If you would like to know when my next release is available and other fun stuff, sign up for my newsletter here: www.annroth.net

THERE ARE 12 sexy firefighter books planned for the **Heroes of Rogue Valley: Calendar Guys**

OTHER BOOKS:
Halo Island:
All I Want for Christmas
The Pilot's Woman
Ooh, Baby!

ANN ROTH CLASSICS:
Father of the Year
A Place to Belong
My Sisters
Another Life

VISIT ME AT FACEBOOK FACEBOOK.COM/ANN-ROTHAUTHORPAGE
Follow me on Twitter @Ann_Roth

Email me at ann@annroth.net
Visit my website www.annroth.net

THANKS, and until next time,
Ann

ALSO BY ANN ROTH

Ann Roth Classics

A Place to Belong

Father of the Year

Another Life

My Sisters

Dunlin Shores

Book 1 Just the Way You Are

Book 2 Wedding Bell Blues

Book 3 Falling for Mr. Wrong

Book 4: A Special Kind of Love

Firefighters

Book 1 Mr. January

Book 2 Mr. February

Book 3 Mr. March

Book 4: Mr. April

Book 5: Mr. May

Book 6: Mr. June

Book 7: Mr. July

Book 8: Mr. August

Book 9: Mr. September

Book 10: Mr. December

Halo Island

Book 1 All I Want for Christmas

Book 2 The Pilot's Woman

Book 3 Ooh, Baby!

Book 4 The One I Love

Miracle Falls

Book 1 Christmas in Miracle Falls

Book 2 Dream a Little Dream

Book 3 It Had to Be You

Book 4: You're the One That I Want

Saddlers Prairie

Book 1 Since I Fell for You

Book 2 I'll Be There

Book 3 Until There Was You

ABOUT THE AUTHOR

Ann Roth is an award-winning author of 40-plus contemporary romance and women's fiction novels, as well as novellas and numerous short stories. Her first novel was published in 2000 by Harlequin Special Edition and was nominated by *Romantic Times* as best first book. Ann lives with the love of her life in the Greater Seattle area and enjoys creating flawed characters and putting them in challenging situations that help them grow and ultimately find love— whether or not they're looking for it.

Find out about new releases!
Sign up for my newsletter

Or visit my website www.annroth.net